LITERATURE & THOUGHT

Flights of Fantasy

Perfection Learning

EDITORIAL DIRECTOR   Julie A. Schumacher

SENIOR EDITOR   Terry Ofner

PERMISSIONS   Laura Pieper

REVIEWER   Jonathan R. Kahle

DESIGN AND PHOTO RESEARCH   William Seabright and Associates,
                            Wilmette, Illinois

COVER ART   I AND THE VILLAGE 1911   Marc Chagall

ACKNOWLEDGMENTS

"Fantasy," from *Asimov's Galaxy: Reflections On Science Fiction* by Isaac Asimov.
Copyright © 1989 by Nightfall, Inc. Used by permission of Doubleday, a division of Random
House, Inc.

"Before I Wake" by Jim Cort. Copyright © 1989 by Jim Cort. First published in *October
Dreams: A Harvest of Horror,* edited by David Kubicek and Jeff Mason (Kubicek &
Associates, 1989). Reprinted by permission of the author.

"Between the Lines" by Ruth Trowbridge. From the *English Journal*, Vol. 64, No. 5.
Copyright© 1975 by the National Council of Teachers of English. Reprinted with permission.

"Black Angel" by Nancy Springer. Taken from *Orphans of the Night* edited by Josepha
Sherman (Walker Publishing). Copyright © 1995 Nancy Springer. Reprinted by permission
of Jean V. Naggar Literary Agency for the author.

"Caleb's Colors" from *Mindquakes: Stories To Shatter Your Brain* by Neal Shusterman.
Copyright © 1996 by Neal Shusterman. Reprinted by permission of St. Martin's Press, LLC.

"The Chaser" by John Collier. Copyright © 1940, renewed 1968 by John Collier.
Reprinted by permission of Harold Matson Co., Inc.

"Disenchantment" from *Burning Bush* by Louis Untermeyer, copyright © 1928 by Harcourt,
Inc. and renewed 1956 by Louis Untermeyer, reprinted by permission of the publisher.

"Fafnir" by Stevie Smith, from *Collected Poems of Stevie Smith*. Copyright © 1972 by
Stevie Smith. Reprinted by permission of New Directions Publishing Corp.
CONTINUED ON PAGE 151

Why Read Fantasy?

*T*he question above is the *essential question* that you will consider as you read this book. The literature, activities, and organization of the book will lead you to think critically about this question, to understand the elements of fantasy writing, and, perhaps, to become one of the millions of avid fantasy readers around the world.

To help you shape your answer to the broad essential question, you will read and respond to four sections, or clusters. Each cluster addresses a specific question and thinking skill.

CLUSTER ONE What is a fantasy? **DEFINE**

CLUSTER TWO What can fantasy teach us? **ANALYZE**

CLUSTER THREE What's real and how do you know? **EVALUATE**

CLUSTER FOUR Thinking on your own **SYNTHESIZE**

Notice that the final cluster asks you to think independently about your answer to the essential question—*Why read fantasy?*

Fantasy

I think if I should wait some night in an enchanted forest
With tall dim hemlocks and moss-covered branches,
And quiet, shadowy aisles between the tall blue-lichened trees;
With low shrubs forming grotesque outlines in the moonlight,
And the ground covered with a thick carpet of pine needles
So that my footsteps made no sound,—

They would not be afraid to glide silently from their hiding places
To the white patch of moonlight on the pine needles,
And dance to the moon and the stars and the wind.

Their arms would gleam white in the moonlight
And a thousand dewdrops sparkle in the dimness of their hair;
But I should not dare to look at their wildly beautiful faces.

RUTH MATHER SKIDMORE

Flights of Fantasy

TABLE OF CONTENTS

The Snake That Swallowed Its Tail

$\mathcal{O}$nce upon a time (in 1865, to be more exact), a German chemist named Friedrich August Kekulé von Stradonitz was sitting beside his fireplace. He drifted off to sleep and had a dream. Accounts of Kekulé's dream vary, but in most versions, he saw a snake swallowing its own tail.

As dreams go, Kekulé's may not seem all that remarkable. People dream far stranger things—for example, people dream that they are able to breathe underwater, read people's minds, or fly. In dreams, our wildest fantasies can seem absolutely real.

What is a fantasy, exactly? One dictionary defines it as "the free play of creative imagination." And in the imagination, whether waking or sleeping, impossible things can happen. Of course, you can fantasize about *possible* things easily enough. You can imagine yourself shooting the winning basket in the big game, or getting some cool new clothes. But why stop there? In the privacy of your own fantasies, why not imagine yourself the king or queen of the galaxy?

On the other hand, why bother to fantasize at all? Of what real use are fantasies? Wish fulfillment is one possibility. According to psychiatrist Sigmund Freud, this is why we dream. In waking life, he explained, we are constantly aware of what we *can't* do. Our nighttime dreams offer us an escape from our resulting frustration—and so, it would seem, do our daydreams.

If this is so, it is not surprising that there is such a huge market for wish fulfillment. Our culture swamps us with fantasies in books, television shows, movies, popular songs, and advertisements. People are ready and willing to pay good money to escape from reality.

But does it really make sense to call all dreams and fantasies mere wish fulfillment? For example, what kind of wish does a dream like Kekulé's satisfy? Does anybody really wish that snakes could swallow their tails?

As it happened, Kekulé was pondering a scientific problem before he dozed and dreamed. He had been studying a substance called benzene, which had been discovered in 1825. Benzene had already proven useful as a solvent and a fuel, but nobody understood its molecular makeup.

Molecules are microscopic building blocks of matter. Molecules, in turn, are made out of even smaller particles called atoms. Kekulé was trying to understand the shape of a benzene molecule. How were its atoms arranged?

Kekulé was stumped by this problem—until he had his dream. He awoke with the image of the snake swallowing its tail in his mind. And suddenly, he had his answer. The benzene molecule was shaped like the snake! Its atoms were arranged in a circle!

Many other scientific breakthroughs have arisen from dreams or daydreams. In fact, scientists often speak of fantasy with great respect. As the great physicist Albert Einstein once remarked, "The gift of fantasy has meant more to me than my talent for absorbing positive knowledge."

Indeed, stories like that of Kekulé's dream suggest that fantasy is very useful. Too often, a so-called "realistic" attitude can mean over-looking realities that are right under our noses. In 1901, a brilliant astronomer named Simon Newcomb convincingly argued that machine-powered, human-piloted flight was scientifically impossible. Two years later, Wilbur and Orville Wright flew the first airplane, fueled by untold ages of dreams and fantasies.

Allowing our minds to wander into realms of the impossible can wake us up to unnoticed possibilities. When this happens, fantasy is much more than a form of escape. It is nothing less than a key to discovery.

CREATOR & CREATION

THE BROTHERS GRIMM
Jakob (1785-1863) above left, and Wilhelm (1786-1859) above right. Their collection of folklore known as *Grimm's Fairy Tales* contains such classics as "Hansel and Gretel" and "Little Red Riding Hood."

Lewis Carroll
right, is the pen name for Charles Lutwidge Dodgson (1832-1898). In 1865 he wrote *Alice's Adventures in Wonderland* to entertain a young friend.

J. R. R. Tolkien
(1892-1973) right, British
scholar and novelist.
He created and illustrated
an entire fantasy world
for the characters in *The
Hobbit* and his epic trilogy
The Lord of the Rings.

Alan Alexander Milne
(1882-1956) above. His son,
Christopher Robin, pictured here,
and his son's teddy bear were
the inspiration for *Winnie-the-Pooh*
published in 1926.

Anne McCaffrey
(1926-) right. Dragons
and their riders populate
McCaffrey's imaginary
planet of Pern. Their
adventures are told in a
series of fantasy novels.

11

CONCEPT VOCABULARY

You will find the following terms and definitions useful as you read and discuss the selections in this book.

dragon a mythical creature usually represented as a large, lizard-like monster with lion's claws and scaly skin; generally breathes fire

dwarf a small, legendary, manlike being who is usually misshapen and ugly and skilled as a craftsman

elf an otherworldly being resembling a human. Elves are small, shy, mischievous creatures considered to have magical powers.

fairy a magical, imaginary being generally depicted with wings

fairy tale a story involving fantastic forces and beings such as goblins, fairies, wizards, and trolls

folktale an anonymous and timeless tale originally circulated through oral retellings

gnome a dwarflike creature who lives underground and guards treasures

goblin an ugly and sometimes mischievous creature; usually given to evil

illusion a false view of reality

magic sorcery; to control nature using supernatural means such as charms and spells

monster an imaginary creature with a bizarre or frightening shape or appearance

reality the sum of all that is actual and true

supernatural that which has powers that go beyond the natural laws of science and nature

three wishes a subgenre of folktales in which the protagonist is given three wishes. The crux of the tale is the manner in which the main character "spends" his or her wishes.

transformation the process of changing in form or appearance

troll a supernatural creature that lives in caves or under bridges. Trolls, who first appeared in Scandinavian folklore, may be giant or dwarf, friendly or mischievous.

wish fulfillment state or condition in which every desire or wish is granted

witch one who is credited with supernatural powers

wizard a wise man; one skilled in magic

CLUSTER ONE

WHAT IS A FANTASY?
Thinking Skill DEFINING

FANTASY

ISAAC ASIMOV

$\mathcal{F}$antasy" is from the Greek *phantasia*, which refers to the faculty of imagination. The word is sometimes spelled "phantasy" in homage[1] to Greek, but I find that foolish. (In fact, I find the Greek *ph* foolish altogether and think it would be delightful if we spoke of "fotografs" and "filosofy," as the Italians do.) A contracted form of "fantasy," with a similar meaning, is "fancy."

In a very broad sense, all fiction (and a great deal of nonfiction) is fantasy, in that it is drawn from the imagination. We in our group,[2] however, give the word a special meaning. It is not the plot of a story that makes it a fantasy, however imaginative that plot might be. It is the background against which the plot is played out that counts.

The plot of *Nicholas Nickleby*,[3] for instance, is entirely imaginative. The characters and events existed entirely in Charles Dickens' imagination but the background is the England of the 1830s exactly as it was. This is "realistic fiction." (We can even use the term where the background is made artificially pretty. Surely, the cowboys of real life must have been pretty dirty and smelly, but you'd never think it to look at Gene Autry or Randolph Scott.)[4]

---

1 **homage:** tribute; honor

2 **our group:** the editor and editorial directors of *Issac Asimov Science Fiction Magazine*

3 *Nicholas Nickleby:* a realistic novel by Charles Dickens set in England. The novel exposed the cruel conditions of many schools of the period.

4 **Gene Autry ... Randolph Scott:** television and movie actors who played cowboys

If, on the other hand, the background does not describe any actual background as it is (or once was) then we have "imaginative fiction." Science fiction and fantasy are each an example of imaginative fiction.

If the nonexistent background is one that might conceivably exist someday, given appropriate changes in the level of science and technology, or given certain assumptions that do not conflict with science and technology as we know it today, then we have science fiction.

If the nonexistent background cannot ever exist no matter what *reasonable* changes or assumptions we postulate,[5] then it is fantasy.

To give specific examples, the Foundation series is science fiction, and *The Lord of the Rings* is fantasy. To be more general about it, spaceships and robots are science fiction, while elves and magic are fantasy.

But there are all kinds of fantasy. There is "heroic fantasy" in which the characters are larger than life. In this case, the outsize nature of the characters may be so enormous as to verge on the grotesque,[6] as in the case of Superman or the other superheroes; or the characters may be so human in many ways that we find ourselves accepting them as real, as in the case of the elves and hobbits of Tolkien's masterpiece. The so-called "sword and sorcery" tales [are] a subdivision of this.

There is "legendary fantasy," which deliberately mimics the myth-making activities of an earlier age. We can have modern retellings of the Trojan War, or the voyage of the Argonauts, or the saga of the Ring of the Nibelungen, or of King Arthur and his Knights of the Round Table. A marvelous recent example of this last is Marion Zimmer Bradley's *The Mists of Avalon.*

There is "children's fantasy" of which the well-known "fairy tales" are the best example, though these were definitely adult folk tales to begin with. Modern examples can stretch from the inspired madness of Lewis Carroll's *Alice in Wonderland* to the realism of Hugh Lofting's Dr. Dolittle tales (so realistic we almost forget that animals which talk and think in human fashion are actually fantasy).

There is "horror fantasy" in which tales of ghosts and malign[7] beings such as devils and ghouls and monsters are used to thrill and frighten us. The motion pictures are rich in this type, from the inspired greatness of *King Kong* and *Frankenstein* to the good-natured foolishness of *Godzilla.*

5 **postulate:** theorize; guess

6 **grotesque:** ridiculous; abnormal

7 **malign:** evil; malevolent

And there is "satirical fantasy," such as the marvelous tales of John Collier[8]—and this, frankly, is my favorite type of fantasy.

There may be other types, and numerous subdivisions of each; in fact, you may have a different system of classification altogether. However, the salient facts are that fantasy is a very broad and heterogeneous[9] field of literature, and that every variety can vary in quality from the very good to the very bad.

WISH FULFILLMENT

It seems to me that most fantasy is born of wish fulfillment, and that should be a strong component in its perennial popularity.

After all, the Universe is *not* what we want it to be and from childhood on we desperately wish that were not so.

---

8 **John Collier:** twentieth-century American short story writer. See his short story, "The Chaser" in the second cluster of this book.

9 **heterogeneous:** made of dissimilar or diverse ingredients

FERDINAND LURED BY ARIEL
1849
John Everett Millais

Wouldn't it be wonderful if you were so good-looking that members of the opposite sex would swoon with desire for you? Wouldn't it be great if you were so strong or so skillful at the martial arts that no one would dare cross you, especially that rotten bully down the street? Wouldn't it be marvelous if you could fly by just flapping your hands slightly, or could be invisible if you wanted to be, or could have anything you wanted just by snapping your fingers? Go ahead, make up your own list.

It's not only fantasy that feeds your desires. Modern advertisement offers you wish fulfillment in huge quantities and makes millions as a result. Let a woman but use a particular brand of toothpaste and that handsome fellow, who had earlier been indifferent, becomes instantly enamored. Just place a drop of this ointment on your skin and eternal youth is yours. . . .

Popular songs tell you that wishing will make it so.

You might think that all this is just food for the childish in us, but there are people who find support for wish fulfillment in science, too. "What man can imagine," they intone[10] solemnly, "man can do." And the history of technology offers us many examples.

It has been a millennia-long dream of humanity to fly, and look here—we can fly. We can fly faster and longer than birds. We have built contraptions that can carry hundreds of people through the stratosphere at supersonic speeds. How's that for wish fulfillment?

And we have television, and electric lighting at the touch of a button, and elevators to take us to the top of a tall building, and automobiles that are more convenient than any set of seven-league boots,[11] and anesthetics[12] that do away with pain, and magic potions called "antibiotics" that cure disease, and so on, and so on, and so on. Ask any primitive storyteller to imagine a wish and it is very likely we can point to something in modern technology that would correspond.

Just the same, while science is important as a device that can guide the way to astonishing things made possible, it is even more important as a way of setting *limits*. It marks the impossible.

Sure you can fly by taking advantage of the laws of aerodynamics and by expending sufficient energy, but that's not the way *I* want to fly. *I* want to fly by having my body lift into the air, and move this way and

---

10 **intone:** say; pronounce

11 **seven-league boots:** magical footwear enabling the wearer to take strides of seven leagues (twenty-one miles)

12 **anesthetics:** painkillers

that, quickly or slowly, *without any expenditure of energy on my part*. I want effortless flying without machinery. I can imagine that without any trouble, but I can't do it, and I suspect it will be forever impossible for anyone to do it. The implacability[13] of the law of conservation of energy and the unlikelihood of being able to monkey with the gravitational interaction stand in the way.

What started me thinking in this direction was the premiere of the "Twilight Zone" series on television. It opened with two half-hour dramas. The first was a dramatic version of Harlan Ellison's "Shatterday."

The second, however, is what I want to talk about. It was called *A Little Peace and Quiet* and dealt with a nice woman who had four totally impossible and noisy children, a thickheaded, noisy husband, and a noisy dog. Unfortunately, she found it impossible to impose any sort of order on them. My own idea, as I watched, was a simple and direct one. Kill them all.

However, our heroine found a locket in a box in her backyard. She put it on and then, when driven to distraction by her horrible family, she screamed, "Shut up. Just shut up," and they were all quiet. In fact, they were more than quiet; they all froze. Everything froze, and it became quite apparent that the woman's locket was a device that, at will, could stop time.

Nor was it a local phenomenon, for as the drama proceeded, and she had other opportunities to make use of her new ability, it became perfectly clear that it stopped time for the whole Earth and, very likely, for the whole Universe.

What's more, she could start it again any time by saying, "Start talking."

That amounted to several wish fulfillments at once. She was, of course, invisible to anyone else while time was stopped. She could do anything she wanted, such as lifting something out of another woman's shopping cart, or taking liberties with a very handsome young man who was frozen and helpless. (She didn't, but it was made perfectly clear that she had the impulse to.)

As fantasy, it was fascinating. As science, alas, it was impossible.

But don't get me wrong. I'm not a spoilsport. I enjoyed the drama, and though I might have muttered to my dear wife, Janet, "All this is impossible," I didn't let that interfere with my enjoyment. It's just important not to mistake fantasy for science, that's all. ∾

---

13 **implacability:** rigidity; unchanging nature

Middle Woman

ORSON SCOTT CARD

Ah-Cheu was a woman of the great kingdom of Ch'in, a land of hills and valleys, a land of great wealth and dire poverty. But Ah-Cheu was a middle person, neither rich nor poor, neither old nor young, and her husband's farm was half in the valley and half on the hill. Ah-Cheu had a sister older than her, and a sister younger than her, and one lived thirty leagues[1] to the north, and the other thirty leagues to the south. "I am a middle woman," Ah-Cheu boasted once, but her husband's mother rebuked her, saying, "Evil comes to the middle, and good goes out to the edges."

Every year Ah-Cheu put a pack on her back and journeyed for a visit either to the sister to the north or to the sister to the south. It took her three days to make the journey, for she did not hurry. But one year she did not make the journey, for she met a dragon on the road.

The dragon was long and fine and terrible, and Ah-Cheu immediately knelt and touched her forehead to the road and said, "Oh, dragon, spare my life!"

The dragon only chuckled deep in his throat and said, "Woman, what do they call you?"

Not wishing to tell her true name to the dragon, she said, "I am called Middle Woman."

"Well, Middle Woman, I will give you a choice. The first choice is to have me eat you here in the road. The second choice is to have me grant you three wishes."

---

1 **leagues:** a league is a unit of distance from about 2.4 to 4.6 miles

EQUESTRIENNE (Detail)
Eighth Century
China, Tang Dynasty

Surprised, Ah-Cheu raised her head. "But of course I take the second choice. Why do you set me a problem with such an easy solution?"

"It is more amusing," said the dragon, "to watch human beings destroy themselves than to overpower them quickly."

"But how can three wishes destroy me?"

"Make a wish, and see."

Ah-Cheu thought of many things she might wish for, but was soon ashamed of her greed. "I wish," she finally said, having decided to ask for only what she truly needed, "for my husband's farm to always produce plenty for all my family to eat."

"It shall be done," said the dragon, and he vanished, only to reappear a moment later, smiling and licking his lips. "I have done," he said, "exactly what you asked—I have eaten all your family, and so your husband's farm, even if it produces nothing, will always produce plenty for *them* to eat."

Ah-Cheu wept and mourned and cursed herself for being a fool, for now she saw the dragon's plan. Any wish, however innocent, would be turned against her.

"Think all you like," said the dragon, "but it will do you no good. I have had lawyers draw up legal documents eight feet long, but I have found the loopholes."

Then Ah-Cheu knew what she had to ask for. "I wish for all the world to be exactly as it was one minute before I left my home to come on this journey."

The dragon looked at her in surprise. "That's all? That's all you want to wish for?"

"Yes," said Ah-Cheu. "And you must do it now."

And suddenly she found herself in her husband's house, putting on her pack and bidding good-bye to her family. Immediately she set down the pack.

"I have changed my mind," she said. "I am not going."

Everyone was shocked. Everyone was surprised. Her husband berated her for being a changeable woman. Her mother-in-law denounced her for having forgotten her duty to her sisters. Her children pouted because she had always brought them each a present from her journeys to the north and south. But Ah-Cheu was firm. She would not risk meeting the dragon again.

And when the furor died down, Ah-Cheu was far more cheerful than she had ever been before, for she knew that she had one wish left, the third wish, the unused wish. And if there were ever a time of great need, she could use it to save herself and her family.

One year there was a fire, and Ah-Cheu was outside the house, with her youngest child trapped within. Almost she used her wish, but then thought, Why use the wish, when I can use my arms? And she ducked low, and ran into the house, and saved the boy, though it singed off all her hair. And she still had her son, and she still had her wish.

One year there was a famine, and it looked like all the world would starve. Ah-Cheu almost used her wish, but then thought, Why use the wish, when I can use my feet? And she wandered up into the hills, and came back with a basket of roots and leaves, and with such food she kept her family alive until the Emperor's men came with wagons full of rice. And she still had her family, and she still had her wish.

And in another year there was a great flood, and all the homes were swept away, and as Ah-Cheu and her son's baby sat upon the roof, watching the water eat away the walls of the house, she almost used her wish to get a boat so she could escape. But then she thought, Why use the wish, when I can use my head? And she took up the boards from the roof and walls, and with her skirts she tied them into a raft large enough for the baby, and setting the child upon it she swam away, pushing the raft until they reached high ground and safety. And when her son found her alive, he wept with joy, and said, "Mother Ah-Cheu, never has a son loved his mother more!"

And Ah-Cheu had her posterity, and yet still she had her wish.

And then it was time for Ah-Cheu to die, and she lay sick and frail upon a bed of honor in her son's house, and the women and children and old men of the village came to keen[2] for her and honor her as she lay dying. "Never has there been a more generous, a more godfavored woman!" And she was content to leave the world, because she had been so happy in it.

And on her last night, as she lay alone in darkness, she heard a voice call her name.

"Middle Woman," said the voice, and she opened her eyes, and there was the dragon.

"What do you want with me?" she asked. "I'm not much of a morsel to eat now, I'm afraid."

---

2 **keen:** to lament the death of a loved one by wailing loudly

But then she saw the dragon looked terrified, and she listened to what he had to say.

"Middle Woman," said the dragon, "you have not used your third wish."

"I never needed it."

"Oh, cruel woman! What a vengeance you take! In the long run, I never did you any harm! How can you do this to me?"

"But what am I doing?" she asked.

"If you die, with your third wish unused, then I, too, will die!" he cried. "Maybe that doesn't seem so bad to you, but dragons are usually immortal, and so you can believe me when I say my death would cut me off with most of my life unlived."

"Poor dragon," she said. "But what have I to wish for?"

"Immortality," he said. "No tricks. I'll let you live forever."

"I don't want to live forever," she said. "It would make the neighbors envious."

"Great wealth, then, for your family."

"But they have all they need right now."

"Any wish!" he cried. "Any wish, or I will die!"

And so she smiled, and reached out a frail old hand and touched his supplicating claw, and said, "Then I wish a wish, dragon. I wish that all the rest of your life should be nothing but happiness for you and everyone you meet."

The dragon looked at her in surprise, and then in relief, and then he smiled and wept for joy. He thanked her many times, and left her home rejoicing.

And that night Ah-Cheu also left her home, more subtly than the dragon, and far less likely to return, but no less merrily for all that. ୬

Fafnir

STEVIE SMITH

In the quiet waters
Of the forest pool
Fafnir the dragon
His tongue will cool

His tongue will cool
And his muzzle dip
Until the soft waters lave[1]
His muzzle-tip

Happy the dragon
In the days expended
Before the time had come
   for dragons
To be hounded

Delivered in their simplicity
To the Knights of the
   Advancing Band
Who seeing the simple
   dragon
Must kill him out of hand.

When thy body shall be torn
And thy lofty spirit
Broken into pieces
For a Knight's merit,

When thy life-blood shall
   be spilt
And thy Being mild
In torment and dismay
To Death beguiled[2]

Fafnir, I shall say then,
Thou art better dead
For the Knights have
   burnt thy grass
And thou couldst not
   have fed.

The time has not come yet
But must come soon
Meanwhile happy Fafnir
Take thy rest in
   the afternoon.

Take thy rest
Fafnir while thou mayest
In the long grass
Where thou liest

Happy knowing not
In thy simplicity
That the Knights have come
To do away with thee.

SIEGFRIED WITH THE
CARCAS OF FAFNIR
1911
Arthur Rackham

1 **lave:** wash; bathe
2 **beguiled:** tricked; deceived

BEFORE I WAKE

JIM CORT

FILE #: 774629
SUBJECT: Conklin, David
DATE: 10/26/87
PRESENT: Subject; L. Zanelli.

CONKLIN. Are you a doctor?

ZANELLI. I'm a psychiatrist. I work here at the Department.

CONKLIN. You're a cop?

ZANELLI. I'm a police psychiatrist, Mr. Conklin. My name is Zanelli. Why don't you sit—

CONKLIN. What's that thing for?

ZANELLI. It's just to free me from having to take notes. I can turn it off if you wish. (pause) Mr. Conklin?

CONKLIN. A psychiatrist. You can prescribe medicine, right?

ZANELLI. Are you ill?

CONKLIN. No, I'm . . . Yes . . . I need something to keep me awake.

ZANELLI. Like amphetamines? (pause) Mr. Conklin, according to the arrest report, you entered the Waverly Pharmacy and tried to fill an apparently forged prescription for amphetamines. When the pharmacist refused to honor the prescription you became violent and abusive. (pause) You can have your lawyer present if you wish.

CONKLIN. I don't have a lawyer. I don't need a lawyer. I'm not a criminal.

ZANELLI. Wouldn't you be more comfortable if you sat down?

CONKLIN. Yes, that's why I'm standing. That's why I'm pacing. If I get comfortable I'll fall asleep.

ZANELLI. Why don't you want to fall asleep?

CONKLIN. (laughs) Oh. I want to, more than anything in the world. I've been awake, God it must be four days now. But I can't. I can't let myself.

ZANELLI. Why not?

CONKLIN. Because if I go to sleep I'll die.

ZANELLI. Why do you think that?

CONKLIN. I don't think it, I know it! I know it! You think I'm crazy, don't you? They think I'm crazy; that's why they sent you.

ZANELLI. I don't think anything, Mr. Conklin. Not yet. Tell me why you believe you'll die if you go to sleep.

CONKLIN. I can't answer these questions. I don't have a lot of time. I can't stay awake forever. I need help. I've got to get something. Can't you get something?

ZANELLI. Mr. Conklin, I am trying to help you, but I need more information.

CONKLIN. If I tell you what you want to know, will you get me something to take?

ZANELLI. I can't make any promises. It depends on what I hear.

CONKLIN. All right, all right. I had a dream. A week ago I had a dream. I was in some kind of cell. Not like this one. The walls and floor were stone. They were cold and damp, like a dungeon. It was dark and I was lying on the floor. There were dogs barking somewhere far away. I didn't know how I'd got there or where

I was or anything. After a while I heard footsteps, and the door to the cell opened and two men came in, big guys, all muscle. They grabbed me and dragged me out of the cell and down a long passage. That was all stone, too, and clammy. I tried to talk to them, but they paid no attention. We got to the end of the passageway and came to this big wooden door. One of the men started to open the door, but just as he did, I woke up. It was still night, and my arms were aching, both of them. I had bruises on my arms where those guys were holding me.

ZANELLI. Yes?

CONKLIN. Well, they're gone now. They faded. That was a week ago.

ZANELLI. I see. What happened after that?

CONKLIN. I had the same dream again the next night.

ZANELLI. Tell me about the next night.

CONKLIN. I was back in the cell, the same one. Everything was the same, except I wasn't the same.

ZANELLI. How do you mean?

CONKLIN. I knew where I was. I recognized the place. I knew there was a passage outside the door. And I knew those guys would be coming for me. And they did come for me. They dragged me down that same passage, but when we got to the door I didn't wake up. It went on. One of them opened the door and there was this stone staircase. It looked old. The stairs were all worn down in the middle. They dragged me up the stairs. The barking was growing louder. We got to the top. There was a doorway, and beyond it a huge room. I'd never seen anything like it. It had a high ceiling. There were torches set along the walls. It looked primitive, savage. I tried to break away from the guards. One of them pulled me back and gave me a slap across the face. The barking was very loud; it seemed to echo off the walls. It was still ringing in my ears when I woke up. And when I did wake up, my lip was bleeding.

ZANELLI. You could have done that yourself in your sleep; bitten your lip.

CONKLIN. Sure, I could have. But I didn't. I was there. I was there on the first night, and then they brought me back.

ZANELLI. Who brought you back?

CONKLIN. I don't know! Whoever they are, they can only get at me when I'm asleep. Don't you understand? That's why I can't go to sleep.

ZANELLI. Mr. Conklin, why do you suppose these people, whoever they are—

CONKLIN. Oh, I know that. I found out on the third night. The third night they got me into that big room. There was a pit sunk into the floor in the middle of the room. That was where the barking was coming from. They brought me right up to the edge. There were dogs down there, or wolves. There must have been a dozen of them. They went crazy when they saw me, howling and snapping. The walls of the pit were stone and smeared with something red. I thought I saw bones. And the smell, oh God, the smell. I looked up. There was some kind of balcony looking down on the pit. I could see dark shapes, like people up there watching. Then the guards pushed me forward. They were going to throw me in. I struggled, but it didn't do any good. I felt my foot slipping. I screamed. I woke up screaming, and I went right on screaming. That was the last night I slept. That was four days ago. If I fall asleep again, I'll be in that pit.

ZANELLI. And you haven't slept in four days?

CONKLIN. I tried everything. Drinking coffee till it made me sick; walking all night. I didn't dare sit down. I couldn't go to work. I couldn't do anything. Finally I went to my doctor. I told him the whole story. He just stared at me like I'd sprouted antlers or something. All at once I knew what he was thinking. It had never occurred to me until that moment. It was real to me. I was there, but he didn't believe it. It's only your own dreams that are real, nobody else's. He started to say something, and then the phone rang. While he was talking I took one of his prescription forms and ran out. I didn't know what else to do.

(pause)

You don't believe me either, do you? Look, I'm not asking you to believe me, just . . . just give me the benefit of the doubt, can't you? Get me to a doctor, or give me something to keep me awake, or just send somebody down here to wake me up if I drop off. I can't hold out like this much longer. I need help. Somebody's got to help me.

M E M O

FROM: Leonard Zanelli

DATE: Oct. 28, 1989

TO: Captain W. Petrie,
Homicide Division

SUBJECT: David Conklin

Before I answer your first question, I must point out that my interview with the subject on October 26 of this year (tran-script attached) lasted only fifteen minutes. Any opinion I might express concerning his mental state would have to be tentative, and could only concern his mental condition at the time. I can venture no opinion concerning the subject's general mental health.

Mr. Conklin was in a highly agitated state which, in my opin-ion, could only partially be accounted for by the shock of his arrest and subsequent confinement. He never once sat down or rested the whole time I was present. His constant pacing interfered considerably with the interview process.

The subject also displayed many symptoms of sleep deprivation, including slurred speech, disorientation, and difficulty in concentration.

His refusal to rest in the face of his obvious physical and mental exhaustion is a telling indicator of the overpowering proportions his obsessive fear of sleep had assumed. I would not be prepared to say, however, that Mr. Conklin was insane in any legal sense.

Parenthetically, the possibility should be considered that the subject had been ingesting some form of amphetamine in order to remain awake (although this was not mentioned) and that his supply had run out. Prolonged use of these drugs frequently results in severe mood changes, bizarre behavior, and even hallucinations.[1]

In answer to your second question; although the actions of persons under stress are difficult to predict, there is no doubt that Mr. Conklin believed himself to be in a desperate situation. This belief, coupled with a possibly drug-induced psychosis,[2] could certainly have led to his subsequent suicide.

1 **hallucinations:** seeing objects that are not there

2 **psychosis:** mental illness

MEDICAL EXAMINER'S REPORT

SUMMARY

DATE: Oct 29, 1989   **SUBJECT:** Conklin, D.

CASE # 774629

The subject's body was riddled with multiple puncture wounds, gashes, and lacerations. A complete inventory is included in the full report. Time of death was between 6:00 and 10:00 PM on October 26. Cause of death could have been any of several of these wounds, particularly the severe gashing at the throat. Loss of blood was considerable.

Neither the nature nor the configuration of these wounds is consistent with self-infliction.

Blood analysis shows no trace of any form of medication, however, high levels of caffeine were noted.

The tuft of hair found clutched in the subject's right hand is not human hair, as was first believed, but more closely resembles the fur of a large dog.

Leonard Zanelli
27 Keller Avenue
Winfield, NJ 07098
November 13, 1989

Dr. Alfred Volner
Breismann Psychiatric Institute
Princeton, NJ 08543

Dear Dr. Volner,

I telephoned your office several times, but it seems my messages never reached you. I was hoping you might remember me. I worked under you at Stanford in 1978. All I ask is a few moments of your time. You have been at the forefront of psychiatric research for so many years. Surely you will understand the importance of what I have to tell you.

In the course of my work with the police department here I have encountered a hitherto unknown form of sleep disorder. The symptoms are quite pronounced and become progressively more severe as time goes on. I can find no mention of it anywhere, even in the most obscure sources. I myself know of only two cases, but I can assure you they are both unquestionably authentic.

Dr. Volner, it is vitally important that I work with you to find a treatment for this disorder. The department has granted me a leave of absence, and I can start immediately. I can supply you with all the data you need. Please believe me—it is desperately urgent that a treatment be found.

Drugs are effective, but only up to a point. Before long the level of dosage needed becomes too great to be tolerated. This problem has consumed my every waking moment. As I write this I have not slept at all in 9 days. I am convinced there is some element I have overlooked, but it's become so hard to concentrate. If I could only get those damned dogs to stop barking, I might get some rest, clear my head. But the barking gets louder every day. I just can't get it to stop.

Sir Gawain
and the
Loathly Lady

RETOLD BY BETSY HEARNE

*N*ow if you listen awhile I will tell you a tale of Arthur the King and how an adventure once befell him.

Of all kings and all knights, King Arthur bore away the honor wherever he went. In all his country there was nothing but chivalry,[1] and knights were loved by the people.

One day in spring King Arthur was hunting in Ingleswood with all his lords beside him. Suddenly a deer ran by in the distance and the king took up chase, calling back to his knights, "Hold you still every man, I will chase this one myself!" He took his arrows and bow and stooped low like a woodsman to stalk the deer. But every time he came near the animal, it leapt away into the forest. So King Arthur went a while after the deer, and no knight went with him, until at  last he let fly an arrow and killed the deer. He had raised a bugle to his lips to summon the knights when he heard a voice behind him.

"Well met, King Arthur!"

Though he had not heard anyone approach, the king turned to see a strange knight, fully armed, standing only a few yards away.

---

1 **chivalry:** bravery; courtesy

"You have done me wrong many a year and given away my northern lands," said the strange knight. "I have your life in my hands—what will you do now, King Alone?"

"Sir Knight, what is your name?" asked the king.

"My name is Gromer Somer Joure."

"Sir Gromer, think carefully," said the king. "To slay me here, unarmed as I am, will get you no honor. All knights will refuse you wherever you go. Calm yourself—come to Carlyle and I shall mend all that is amiss."

"Nay," said Sir Gromer, "by heaven, King! You shall not escape when I have you at advantage. If I let you go with only a warning, later you'll defy me, of that I'm sure."

"Spare my life, Sir Gromer, and I shall grant you whatever is in my power to give. It is shameful to slay me here, with nothing but my hunting gear, and you armed for battle."

"All your talking will not help you, King, for I want neither land nor gold, truly." Sir Gromer smiled. "Still . . . if you will promise to meet me here, in the same fashion, on a day I will choose . . ."

"Yes," said the king quickly. "Here is my promise."

"Listen and hear me out. First you will swear upon my sword to meet me here without fail, on this day one year from now. Of all your knights none shall come with you. You must tell me at your coming what thing women most desire—and if you do not bring the answer to my riddle, you will lose your head. What say you, King?"

"I agree, though it is a hateful bargain," said the king. "Now let me go. I promise you as I am the true king, to come again at this day one year from now and bring you your answer."

The knight laughed. "Now go your way, King Arthur. You do not yet know your sorrow. Yet stay a moment—do not think of playing false—for by Mary[2] I think you would betray me."

"Nay," said King Arthur. "You will never find me an untrue knight. Farewell, Sir Knight, and evil met. I will come in a year's time, though I may not escape." The king began to blow his bugle for his knights to find him. Sir Gromer turned his horse and was gone as quickly as he had come, so that the lords found their king alone with the slain deer.

"We will return to Carlyle," said the king. "I do not like this hunting."

2 **by Mary:** an oath or appeal to the Virgin Mary

The lords knew by his countenance that the king had met with some disturbance, but no one knew of his encounter. They wondered at the king's heavy step and sad look, until at last Sir Gawain said to the king, "Sire, I marvel at you. What thing do you sorrow for?"

"I'll tell you, gentle Gawain," said Arthur. "In the forest as I pursued the deer, I met with a knight in full armor, and he charged me I should not escape him. I must keep my word to him or else I am foresworn."[3]

"Fear not my lord. I am not a man that would dishonor you."

"He threatened me, and would have slain me with great heat, but I spoke with him since I had no weapons."

"What happened then?" said Gawain.

"He made me swear to meet him there in one year's time, alone and unarmed. On that day I must tell him what women desire most, or I shall lose my life. If I fail in my answer, I know that I will be slain without mercy."

"Sire, make good cheer," said Gawain. "Make your horse ready to ride into strange country, and everywhere you meet either man or woman, ask of them the answer to the riddle. I will ride another way, and every man and woman's answer I will write in a book."

"That is well advised, Gawain," said the king. They made preparations to leave immediately, and when both were ready, Gawain rode one way and the king another—each one asked every man and woman they found what women most desire.

Some said they loved beautiful clothes; some said they loved to be praised; some said they loved a handsome man; some said one, some said another. Gawain had so many answers that he made a great book to hold them, and after many months of traveling he came back to court again. The king was there already with his book, and each looked over the other's work. But no answer seemed right.

"By God," said the king, "I am afraid. I will seek a little more in Ingleswood Forest. I have but one month to my set day, and I may find some good tidings."

"Do as you think best," said Gawain, "but whatever you do, remember that it is good to have spring again."

---

3 **foresworn:** untrue to one's word or oath

King Arthur rode forth on that day, into Ingleswood, and there he met with a lady. King Arthur marveled at her, for she was the ugliest creature that he had ever seen. Her face seemed almost like that of an animal, with a pushed-in nose and a few yellowing tusks for teeth. Her figure was twisted and deformed, with a hunched back and shoulders a yard broad. No tongue could tell the foulness of that lady. But she rode gaily on a palfrey[4] set with gold and precious stones, and when she spoke her voice was sweet and soft.

"I am glad that I have met with you, King Arthur," she said. "Speak with me, for your life is in my hand. I know of your situation, and I warn you that you will not find your answer if I do not tell you."

"What do you want with me, lady?" said the king, taken aback by the lady's boldness.

"Sir, I would like to speak with you. You will die if I do not save you, I know it very well."

"What do you mean, my lady, tell me," stammered the king. "What is your desire, why is my life in your hand? Tell me, and I shall give you all you ask."

"You must grant me a knight to wed," said the lady slowly. "His name is Sir Gawain. I will make this bargain: if your life is saved another way, you need not grant my desire. If my answer saves your life, grant me Sir Gawain as my husband. Choose now, for you must soon meet your enemy."

"By Mary," said the king, "I cannot grant you Sir Gawain. That lies with him alone—he is not mine to give. I can only take the choice to Sir Gawain."

"Well," she said. "Then go home again and speak to Sir Gawain. For though I am foul, yet am I merry, and through me he may save your life or ensure your death."

"Alas!" cried the king. "That I should cause Gawain to wed you, for he will not say no. I know not what I should do."

"Sir King, you will get no more from me. When you come again with your answer I will meet you here."

"What is your name, I pray you tell me?"

---

4 **palfrey:** riding horse

"Sir King, I am the Dame Ragnell, that never yet betrayed a man."

"Then farewell, Dame Ragnell," said the king.

Thus they departed, and the king returned to Carlyle again with a heavy heart. The first man he met was Sir Gawain. "Sire, how did you fare?" asked the knight.

"Never so ill," said the king. "I fear I will die at Sir Gromer's hand."

"Nay," said Gawain. "I would rather die myself I love you so."

"Gawain, I met today with the foulest lady that I ever saw. She said she would save my life, but first she would have you for her husband."

"Is this all?" asked Gawain. "Then I shall wed her and wed her again! Though she were a fiend, though she were as foul as Beelzebub,[5] her I shall marry. For you are my king and I am your friend—it is my part to save your life, or else I am a false knight and a great coward. If she were the most loathsome woman that ever a man might see, for your love I would spare nothing."

"Thank you Gawain," said King Arthur then. "Of all knights that I have found, you are the finest. You have saved my life, and my love will not stray from you, as I am king in this land."

*C*he day soon came when the king was to meet the Dame Ragnell and bear his answer to Sir Gromer. Gawain rode with him to the edge of Ingleswood Forest, but there the king said, "Sir Gawain, farewell. I must go west, and you must go no further."

"God speed you on your journey. I wish I rode your way," said Gawain.

The king had ridden but a mile or so more when he met the Dame Ragnell. "Ah, Sir King, you are welcome here bearing your answer."

"Now," said the king, "since it can be no other way, tell me your answer, save my life, and Gawain shall you wed; so he has promised. Tell me in all haste. Have done, I may not tarry."

"Sire," said the Dame Ragnell, "now you will know what women desire most, high and low. Some men say we desire to be fair, or to wed,

---

5 **Beelzebub:** the devil

or to remain fresh and young, or to have flattery from men. But there is one thing that is every woman's fantasy: we desire of men, above all other things, to have sovereignty,[6] for then all is ours. Therefore go on your way, Sir King, and tell that knight what I have said to you. He will be angry and curse the woman who told you, for his labor is lost. Go forth—you will not be harmed."

The king rode forth in great haste until he came to the set place and met with Sir Gromer.

"Come, come, Sir King," said the knight sternly. "Now let me have your answer, for I am ready."

The king pulled out the two books for Sir Gromer to see. "Sir, I dare say the right one is there."

Sir Gromer looked over them, every one, and said at last, "Nay, nay, Sir King, you are a dead man."

"Wait, Sir Gromer," said the king. "I have one more answer to give."

"Say it," said Sir Gromer, "or so God help me you shall bleed."

"Now," said the king, "here is my answer and that is all—above all things, women desire sovereignty, for that is their liking and their greatest desire; to rule over any man. This they told me."

Sir Gromer was silent a moment with rage, but then he cried out, "And she that told you, Sir Arthur, I pray to God I might see her burn in a fire, for that was my sister, Dame Ragnell. God give her shame— I have lost much labor. Go where you like, King Arthur, for you are spared. Alas that I ever saw this day, for I know that you will be my enemy and hunt me down."

"No," said King Arthur, "you will never find me an attacker. Farewell." King Arthur turned his horse into the forest again. Soon he met with the Dame Ragnell, in the same place as before. "Sir King," she said. "I am glad you have sped well. I told you how it would be, and now since I and none other have saved your life, Gawain must wed me."

"I will not fail in my promise," said the king. "If you will be ruled by my council, you shall have your will."

"No, Sir King, I will not be ruled," said the lady. "I know what you are thinking. Ride before, and I will follow to your court. Think how I have saved your life and do not disagree with me, for if you do you will be shamed."

6 **sovereignty:** to hold power or authority over others

The king was ashamed to bring the loathly lady openly to the court, but forth she rode till they came to Carlyle. All the country wondered when she came, for they had never seen so foul a creature, but she would spare no one the sight of her. Into the hall she went, saying, "Arthur, King, fetch in Sir Gawain, before all the knights, so that you may troth[7] us together. Set forth Gawain my love, for I will not wait."

Sir Gawain stepped forward then, and said, "Sir, I am ready to fulfill the promise I made to you."

"God have mercy," said the Dame Ragnell when she saw Gawain. "For your sake I wish I were a fair woman, for you are of such good will." Then Sir Gawain wooed her as he was a true knight, and Dame Ragnell was happy.

"Alas!" said the Queen Guinevere, and all the ladies in her bower.[8] "Alas!" said both king and knights, that the beautiful Gawain should wed such a foul and horrible woman.

She would be wedded in no other way than this—openly, with announcements in every town and village, and she had all the ladies of the land come to Carlyle for the feast. The queen begged Dame Ragnell to be married in the early morning, as privately as possible. "Nay," said the lady. "By heaven I will not no matter what you say. I will be wedded openly, as the king promised. I will not go to the church until high-mass time, and I will dine in the open hall, in the midst of all the court."

At the wedding feast there were lords and ladies from all estates, and Dame Ragnell was arrayed in the richest manner—richer even than Queen Guinevere. But all her rich clothes could not hide her foulness. When the feasting began, only Dame Ragnell ate heartily, while the knights and squires sat like stones. After the wedding feast, Sir Gawain and the Lady Ragnell retired to the wedding chamber that had been prepared for them.

"Ah, Gawain," said the lady. "Since we are wed, show me your courtesy and come to bed. If I were fair you would be joyous—

7 **troth:** marry

8 **bower:** a lady's private chamber in a medieval castle

yet for Arthur's sake kiss me at least."

Sir Gawain turned to the lady, but in her place was the loveliest woman that he had ever seen.

"By God, what are you?" cried Gawain.

"Sir, I am your wife, surely. Why are you so unkind?"

"Lady, I am sorry," said Gawain. "I beg your pardon, my fair madam. For now you are a beautiful lady, and today you were the foulest woman that ever I saw. It is well, my lady, to have you thus." And he took her in his arms and kissed her with great joy.

"Sir," she said, "you have half-broken the spell on me. Thus shall you have me, but my beauty will not hold. You may have me fair by night and foul by day, or else have me fair by day, and by night ugly once again. You must choose."

"Alas!" said Gawain, "the choice is too hard—to have you fair on nights and no more, that would grieve my heart and shame me. Yet if I desire to have you fair by day and foul by night I could not rest. I know not in the world what I should say, but do as you wish. The choice is in your hands."

"Thank you, courteous Gawain," said the lady. "Of all earthly knights you are blessed, for now I am truly loved. You shall have me fair both day and night, and ever while I live as fair. For I was shaped by witchcraft by my stepmother, God have mercy on her. By enchantment I was to be the foulest creature, till the best knight of England had wedded me and had given me the sovereignty of all his body and goods. Kiss me, Sir Gawain—be glad and make good cheer, for we are well." The two rejoiced together and thanked God for their fortune.

EMILIA IN HER GARDEN
1454–55
Hours of the Duke of Burgundy

King Arthur came himself to call them to breakfast the next day, wondering why Gawain stayed so late with his loathly bride. Sir Gawain rose, taking the hand of his lady, and opened the door to greet the king.

The Dame Ragnell stood by the fire, with pale lovely skin and red hair spilling down to her knees. "Lo," said Gawain to the king, "this is my wife the Dame Ragnell, who once saved your life." And Gawain told the king the story of the lady's enchantment.

"My love shall she have, for she has been so kind," said the king. And the queen said, "You have my love forever, Lady, for you have saved my Lord Arthur." And from then on, at every great feast, that lady was the fairest, and all his life Gawain loved the Lady Ragnell.

Thus ends the adventure of King Arthur and of the wedding of Sir Gawain. ❧

RESPONDING TO CLUSTER ONE

WHAT IS A FANTASY?

Thinking Skill DEFINING

1. What do you think the dragon would have done if the Middle Woman had wished for help during one of the three disasters: the fire, the famine, or the flood? You will have to make up both Middle Woman's wish and the dragon's action.

2. The **theme** of a piece of literature is the message the writer wishes to convey to the reader. In your opinion, what is the theme of "Fafnir"? Hint: You may find it helpful to first restate the poem in everyday language.

3. In the article "Fantasy," Isaac Asimov suggests the following categories for fantasy: Heroic, Sword/Sorcery, Legendary, Children's, Horror, and Satirical. **Classify** the selections in this cluster using Asimov's terms or your own. Some pieces may fit into more than one category. (Keep your work for use later in this book.)

Title	Types of Fantasy
Middle Woman	
Fafnir	
Before I Wake	
Sir Gawain and the Loathly Lady	

4. In the article "Fantasy," Isaac Asimov lists several wish fulfillments, such as being fantastically good looking, or being able to fly by flapping your arms. Create your own list of things you would wish for if you were given three wishes.

Writing Activity: Defining a Fantasy

Using the classifications from Question 3 above and your own ideas, create your own personal definition of fantasy fiction. Your responses to the questions below might be helpful in composing your essay.

• What elements are needed to create a fantasy?

• What is the purpose and appeal of fantasy fiction?

• How is fantasy different from other popular genres?

A Strong Definition

• begins by stating the term to be defined

• lists the various characteristics or qualities of the term

• provides examples

• ends with a final definition

CLUSTER TWO

WHAT CAN FANTASY TEACH US?

Thinking Skill ANALYZING

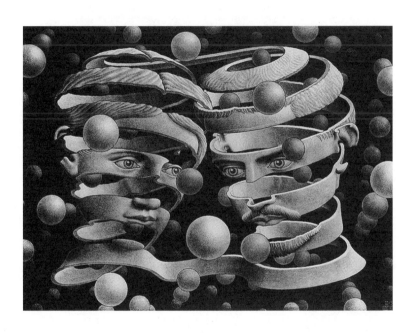

PLAIN MAGIC

TAMORA PIERCE

Only once in my life was I glad that my family was large. Until I was fourteen the tale of my days was one of hand-me-down clothes and toys that barely lasted a month by the time they reached me, and a place to spread my blankets on the floor between my older sisters' beds. Then came the news that the dragon that had been destroying towns to the north was just two days' flight away.

It was time to pack. Everyone had to choose what might be carried to the caves in the mountains and what must be left behind.

With a houseful of frightened older girls and their children—my sisters were married, living with us until their men could build homes of their own—my mother had no use for me. After she had ordered me out of the way for the third time, she thrust bread and cheese into my hands and told me to go.

"Don't stray from the village," she ordered. "Who knows where that dragon is?"

I thought that we would know if he was near, since he was supposed to be as big as three bulls, but nobody argued with my mother. I put my food in a string bag and left our house.

At first I thought I would go to the woods, as I liked to do, but my father saw me and told me to stay close to home. Then I went in search of my friends. All of them had been put to work packing, getting ready to run when the dragon came. Bored and lonely, I wandered into the village and found an unexpected arrival. A peddler had come and had set up in the square across from the fountain.

Her cart was scarlet with designs picked out in yellow paint on the wheels. One whole side of the cart was lowered to form a broad tray. On it were neatly stacked goods: bolts of cloth in a dozen colors, neat rolls of beautiful lace, cloth dolls as small as my fingers or as big as my hand, spools of thread, and balls of yarn. The peddler had placed a wooden bench next to the tray. She sat there, busily embroidering a square of cloth.

She wasn't much to look at—brown and dry and thin, with dark hair tied back under a scarf. Her dress was plain brown cotton with small, dark buttons. She wore skirts as short as a girl my age, hanging just a few inches below the knee. They revealed scuffed, flat-heeled boots, as well-worn and dusty as everything else about her. I guessed her age at a little over thirty.

There was a dragon coming, maybe, but it was still my lucky day. Normally my parents frowned on my speaking to people who came from the big world outside our village, but they were busy. I could talk to this stranger all I wanted.

I told her my name, Tonya. She gave me hers, Lindri. I asked about what she had to sell, and she answered. She even showed me the silks she kept tucked away in the cart, for customers with fatter purses than our villagers had. The silks came from odd-sounding places, where the dyes were ten times more vivid than any we had. Lindri had been to those lands. She described them so beautifully I could almost see them.

She embroidered as she talked. Her needle darted through the cloth as if it were alive, shaping a garden of flowers on what would be a sleeve. I had never been very interested in needlework, but Lindri made it seem fascinating. I didn't realize I was staring at the design until she patted my cheek smartly, waking me from a daze.

"Don't watch so long," she said with a grin. "They say there's a plain kind of magic in needlework—do you want to end up a slave to it, like me?"

I winced. "Don't talk of magic or slavery to me," I growled. "I've no idea of what I'm doing, but people here still keep asking me for charms for everything under the sun."

Lindri raised her brows. "You have magic?"

I nodded.

"Surely your teacher is showing you how to work."

I laughed, bitterness choking me. "Wizard Halen? It's like pulling teeth to get him to teach me what little I *do* know. He's so afraid I'll be better than him that he won't even teach me to read."

We continued to talk about non-magical things. When the noon hour came, I shared my bread and cheese with Lindri, who added some apples, jam made of a berry I had never tasted before, and mugs of cider.

While we ate, four-year-old Krista emerged from her house across the square. Bit by bit she wandered closer as we finished our meal. At last she reached the lowered tray. She stared at the brightly colored balls of yarn, with her finger in her half-open mouth, as if the balls held the answer to some great secret.

Lindri smiled at her. "Hello, young one. Can I do something for you?"

Krista was shy. She turned to run, stumbled, and fell with a shriek. When I picked her up, I had to bite my lip to keep from gasping. She had cut her palm on a rock in the street. The bones of her hand showed through the deep, ugly gash.

"Hush, hush." Lindri took the screaming Krista from me, brushing her off with an efficient hand. "So much noise. Let me see."

To my surprise, Krista stopped wailing. She held the bleeding hand up for Lindri to examine. Blood welled thickly from the cut, and I shivered with fear. Rot was almost impossible to avoid with such a deep wound. The chances were that pretty Krista would lose her hand.

"That's bad, I suppose," Lindri said. "But it could be a lot worse." She took the girl to a water barrel fixed to the rear of the cart, holding Krista's hand beneath the spout as she rinsed the wound clean. She whisked a strip of linen from the piles on the tray and sat down, settling Krista in her lap.

"If you're brave about this," Lindri told her, "you may have one of the red balls of yarn for your very own."

Krista stuck the fingers of her good hand in her mouth and held out the injured hand. Lindri bandaged the cut neatly and quickly. She finished by tying the loose ends in an oddly shaped knot directly over the wound, tapping the knot lightly with her fingers when she was done.

"All fixed," she told Krista, putting a crimson ball of yarn into the child's good hand. "Keep the bandage clean, mind. When you take it off, you'll be as good as new."

As Krista ran home I frowned at Lindri. It would be rude for me to say so to an adult, but I thought it was cruel for Lindri to lie to Krista. The child would know it was a lie when she could no longer use the hand, or worse, was forced to have it cut off.

Lindri smiled at me. "You'll see that I'm right," she said, as if she knew what I had been thinking. "Now, tell me about the dragon who's been preying on this valley."

No one could have disobeyed the soft note of command in Lindri's voice. "It first attacked villages below the northern mountains," I began. "That was about two weeks ago. It's been coming south ever since. It doesn't burn every town in its way, but it's burned enough. People who flee it come through here because we're the last village before the pass out of the valley. But you'd know that if you came up from the south."

"That's right," Lindri replied. "I drove through the pass this morning."

Mistress Fane, the miller's wife, came up to us and pointed to a bolt of cloth. "I'd like to see more of that, if you please," she ordered Lindri. The woman could never ask for anything politely.

"No one knows why it burns some villages and not others," I went on as Mistress Fane inspected another bolt of cloth, and a third. "It was spotted near here two days ago, but we don't know if it'll attack us or not. Everyone hopes it will just go away."

Mistress Fane bought the pink cloth she had been looking at, which filled me with glee. She looked awful in pink.

Lindri picked up her embroidery again. "Why are your people still here?"

"We're too poor," I told her. It felt odd to say such things to a stranger—I was very proud—but Lindri had a listening way about her. I went on as I watched her needle flash through her cloth. "All most of us have is our farms. We can't take them with us, and we've no money to start fresh someplace else." I sighed. "I'd *like* to start someplace else."

Lindri glanced at me. "Adventurous, are you, Tonya?"

I felt as if she'd taken a leash off my tongue. Out spilled my dreams of leaving the valley someday, of seeing new lands and meeting new people, of simply being somewhere *different*. Then I remembered. I was Tonya, the headman's daughter. The only place I was likely to go to was my future husband's home. It was silly to talk of my dreams to Lindri, who had seen the world beyond the mountains. It was silly and it was senseless, because soon she would leave, and I would still be here.

"Where are you going now?" I asked.

She looked at the sun, which slid toward the western horizon, and traded her embroidery for knitting. "North," she replied briefly. "To the mountains, I expect."

"You can't!" I protested, shocked. "It's dangerous. Wild animals live there. More dragons, and bears taller than a tall man, and giant cats—"

Lindri shrugged. "I like animals. They rarely bother you unless you bother them first."

I was about to argue further when Riv interrupted us. He had come in early from putting his sheep up for the night, probably to get news of the dragon. "Excuse me," he said politely, picking up a small square of folded lace. "I want to know how much this is."

Lindri looked him over. "One silver minim."

"For just this little bit?" Riv asked, eyeing the lace. It was beautiful, filmy white stuff. I had an idea that the price Lindri had given him was less than what she would charge somewhere else. He handed the square to her. "Hold this, please? I want to look at the rest." He went to the small stacks of lace at the far end of the tray.

"He seems like a nice young man," Lindri remarked softly. "What can you tell me about him?"

"He's getting married next month," I whispered, keeping an eye on Riv. "His girl Aura is my best friend. She's standing over by the fountain, the one with the basket on her arm. Riv's chief shepherd, but he hasn't been chief through a spring shearing, so he hasn't any money. And all Aura ever wanted was a lace veil when she marries, like the city ladies have."

Lindri was tugging on the edges of the lace Riv had given her, which worried me. What if she got it dirty?

"Nobody else here got a lace veil," I went on. "So people say Aura thinks she's better than everyone else. But it's not true! She just wants something pretty."

Riv came back. "See anything you'd rather have?" Lindri asked.

He offered her a silver minim, his face beet-colored with shame. "No. This is fine." He was trying to smile, but it didn't look right. "It isn't a whole veil, but—well, it's very pretty," he finished.

Lindri pocketed the coin and gave Riv the folded square. "Enjoy it," she told Riv, smiling. "And may your marriage be happy."

Boys had come to set torches around the square. The whole village would be coming here soon, to get the latest news of the dragon. As the torches caught, they threw their wavering light over Riv as he walked back to Aura.

"It's just not fair," I muttered as he offered her the lace. "Old, mean people like Miller Fane and his wife have nice things, but Aura and Riv—"

Riv fumbled the lace and caught it just in time. Then the lace began to unfold, and I gasped. Length after length spilled from Riv's hands like a waterfall, shimmering white in the glow from the torches. Riv had to raise his hands higher and higher to keep the white stuff from touching the ground, while Aura laughed and cried at the same time.

They tried to make Lindri take it back, but she refused. "That's the piece you bought," she told Riv firmly. "Ask Tonya if it ever left my hands after you gave it to me."

And that was the biggest puzzle of all. I had talked to her the whole time, and the only thing she did with that lace was tug on it. I *knew* it had been a folded square of one or two thicknesses when Riv selected it, but I couldn't prove it. They went away at last, Aura crying on Riv's shoulder as he carefully refolded the lace.

Lindri shook her head, straightening the goods on her tray. "People should inspect strange goods carefully," she murmured. "They never know what they've purchased, otherwise."

I was about to ask what Riv *had* bought when my father came as the village headman to meet Lindri. The other two elders, Priest Rand and my teacher, Wizard Halen, soon joined us. As Rand said polite things to Lindri, Halen started to inspect her wares. Suddenly he picked up a square of linen. "There is something odd about this piece," he began.

Lindri snatched it from his fingers. "Don't touch unless you plan to buy," she snapped. "No one buys dirty goods."

Wizard Halen's eyes narrowed. He was about to speak when my brother Selm galloped into the square. Normally Selm was calm and slow-going, but when he reined up before our father, he was in as much of a lather as his horse.

"I saw it settle on Tower Rock!" he gasped. "Long and bronze, like we were told!"

People came quickly to the square as the word spread until everyone was there, including my entire family, Riv, Aura, my other friends, and Krista and her parents. Miller Fane and his wife arrived with their horse-drawn cart—the only one in the village—piled high with their things. They could afford to run, to start fresh somewhere else.

Everyone listened as my father, the priest, and the wizard explained the problem for what seemed like the thousandth time. Were there any choices but flight?

Wizard Halen said, "I may have found a way."

"Tell us, then," Tanner Clyd yelled.

Just then Krista's mother saw the bandage on her girl's hand was dirty and bedraggled. I watched her tug at the strange knot Lindri had used. At last she gave up trying to undo the knot and cut it with her belt knife.

"I have read the various remedies for a plague of dragons," Halen said loudly. His squeaky voice quavered with the effort.

Of course, I thought unhappily. He's been at his precious books. We had fought so often over his teaching me to read that I had finally given up asking.

Halen went on, "A spear made of silver, of course, wielded by a virtuous man—"

Someone called, "If there was enough silver here to make a spear, Wizard, you'd have had it all by now."

My father scowled. "The wizard is trying to aid us," he said. "Listen to him."

Halen looked smug. "A dragon may also be lured to its death in a pit of fire, or buried in a river of ice." He tugged his nose for a moment. "But there is a fourth way to placate a dragon, and I have found it at last."

"Is it as impossible as the others?" Miller Fane wanted to know. "There are no pits of fire or rivers of ice here!"

People muttered agreement. Halen waited until they were quiet before he replied, "It is not impossible, but it is costly. You may think it better to flee."

"Where will we go?" Krista's mother cried. She stopped unwinding the bandage from her daughter's palm. "We have lived here for generations! No one has the coin to build new homes!"

Everyone shouted agreement.

"You must give the dragon something," Halen announced. "You must assuage his hunger."

"Oh, no," Lindri whispered tiredly.

I missed Halen's next words because I was staring at Krista. Her mother had the bandage off at last. She was turning the little one's palm back and forth in the torchlight, trying to see the cut. So was I. The ugly gash that had marred Krista's hand when Lindri bandaged it was gone.

". . . a young girl," I heard Wizard Halen say. "Unmarried. A virgin."

Everyone was silent. To offer the beast one of our own . . . A woman began to cry.

"You must draw lots," Halen went on. "You must be fair."

"Drivel." Everyone turned to stare at Lindri, who stood beside her cart, hands on hips. "Absolute nonsense. Do you seriously think a dragon can taste the difference between a virgin and an old man?"

"You are a stranger here," Miller Fane called. "Speak to our wizard with respect."

"Your wizard doesn't know what he's talking about," Lindri told him calmly and clearly. "Dragons hate the taste of human flesh."

"Legend is filled with the sacrifices made to dragons!" Halen was turning red. Just when he had everyone's attention and respect, this peddler-woman was trying to make him look like a fool.

"Of course they'll eat a human if a human is staked out like a goat," Lindri replied. "They aren't very smart. This one will eat your virgin, and then he'll be sick. A dragon flames only when he is ill. He'll pass over your homes because he has fed, and then he'll burn the next village he sees to the ground. You will have killed a girl needlessly, and others will die or lose their homes. All for the lack of a little sense on your part, *wizard*."

My father was dark with anger. "You have said more than enough," he told Lindri. "You are a guest, and Halen is an elder. Be silent, or our young men will see you on your way."

Lindri eyed my father for a moment, as if she could see through his face into his head. I was angry and ashamed. *I* knew what he was like, but he was my father. What right did a stranger have to look at him as if he were a fool?

Lindri shrugged and sat down. My father stared at us, waiting for another sign of rebellion, then turned to Halen. "How young must they be?"

The wizard swelled with pride. Lindri had been silenced, and now everyone waited for him to tell us what to do. "They must be of marriageable age, and no younger than twelve," he announced.

There were just seven girls of that age—the village was very small. We seven were separated from the others as Carpenter Daws cut a rod into six long pieces and a short one. The wizard made a bag out of my mother's shawl, and the pieces were dumped inside. The priest said a prayer. Then we were told to each step up and take a piece of wood without looking. Lindri was silent, knitting busily.

I got the short piece. When I held it up, everyone looked at my father. They wanted to see if he would try to save me, either because I was his daughter or because after Halen I was the best magic worker in the village. They didn't know my father. I wish *I* hadn't known him as well as I did.

My mother was sobbing quietly. My sisters gathered around her and led her home. Not one of them met my eyes. I looked for my brothers and brothers-in-law in the crowd. They, too, looked away.

"Tonya is the one," my father said. "We will take her to the north meadow tomorrow and leave her there for the dragon."

Aura ran up to me and hugged me fiercely, weeping. I felt distant and strange, as I had since I had seen that short piece of wood. When Riv kissed my cheek and drew Aura away from me, I felt numbly glad. I knew I ought to say something, to them or the elders or someone, but I couldn't think.

Lindri came up to me and put a hand on my shoulder. "You're brave, Tonya," she whispered. "Be brave a while more." She returned to her cart, climbing inside and closing the door behind her.

My father, along with two of my brothers, took me to a shed by the north meadow for the rest of the night. Selm was the one who hesitated when they would have closed the door and locked me in.

"We don't want to do this," he said, almost as if he were pleading with me. "You're my sister, and I—" He seemed to think the better of telling me he loved me. "We have to do this," he told me, hanging his head. "We've no choice." He closed the door. I heard the bolt slide home.

I lay awake all night, staring at the shadowy roof and listening to the men who guarded the shed. None of this felt real, not even the rocks that pressed into my back.

At last I could see bits of pale light through the cracks in the walls. My father, Halen, and Priest Rand came for me.

The post was already standing in the middle of the north meadow. They had found shackles somewhere and hung them from the post. The priest locked them around my hands, muttering a fast prayer as he kept an eye on distant Tower Rock. When a touch of sun showed over the horizon, they left me at the run and hid in the woods at the meadow's edge.

My numbness evaporated. Giddy with sudden fright, I faced Tower Rock and the humped form that sat on top of it. Once the monster's in the air, I thought, he'll be here fast. It'll be over before I can feel it.

At least, I prayed it would be so.

Then I heard the jingle of a horse's harness, the clop of hooves, and the creak of wood. Lindri stopped her cart a little way from me, and her piebald gelding[1] put his head down to graze. The elders yelled for her to get away from me, but they were too afraid to leave the protection of the trees to stop her.

Baffled, I stared at Lindri as she walked over to me. Little things about her struck me as suddenly very important. She was wearing a clean blue dress with white embroideries, and she had wiped yesterday's dust off her boots. She glanced at Tower Rock, her eyes as clear and alert as if she'd been up for hours. As the distant dragon unfurled its wings, Lindri gathered my shackles in her hands.

"This has gone far enough," she said, looking the chains over. "If they'd listened to me, you would have been spared a very bad night. I'm sorry for that."

She tapped each lock with her fingers, just as she had tapped the knot on Krista's bandage. The shackles sprang open. Then she pulled a length of twine from her pocket. "Go, Tonya. I'll tend to the dragon."

It was all too strange. I should have been frightened and hysterical. Instead I quivered with excitement. I went only as far as her cart to wait, stroking the piebald's nose and warming my cold hands in his mane. My father and the others were still shouting. I ignored them, just as Lindri had.

---

1 **piebald gelding:** a neutered male horse with black and white spots or blotches

She faced north, looking just as calm as she had while we gossiped the day before. Only her fingers moved, tying multitudes of knots in her twine. They formed clumps that grew far greater than the amount of string I had seen her take out. Like Riv's lace, the knots spilled from her working hands to the ground in billows. As the dragon leaped into the air from Tower Rock, Lindri bent, gathered the masses of knots into her hands, and straightened.

I glanced back at the woods. Wizard Halen screamed curses, jumping up and down in a fury. My father was staring at Lindri, white-faced. The priest had fallen to his knees and was muttering prayers.

I turned in time to see the dragon as it glided low over the meadow, claws outstretched. Lindri waited until he was directly overhead. She crouched, then leaped, hurling her bundle of knots into the air. They spread until I could see clearly she had shaped a huge net. Like a living thing the net wrapped itself around the dragon, wings, snout, claws and all. The great lizard screeched with alarm as it tumbled to the ground, landing with a thump on the meadow.

As I looked on, the net drew itself tighter and tighter, pulling the dragon's limbs and wings close to its body. It was beautiful, long, and muscular, with copper-bronze scales, gold claws, and deep amber eyes. It was as long as two bulls and as big around as one—a far cry from the three-bull size that people had claimed for it. Pressing its wings against the clinging net, it cried softly, until I began to feel sorry for the thing that might have eaten me.

Lindri approached, tugging a fresh length of twine until it was a rope. Reaching through the net, she slid her rope around the dragon's neck, making a leash. The dragon stopped its struggle, rubbing its muzzle against Lindri's hands. She spoke to it quietly before she pulled her hands free of the net. Now the creature sat and waited, eyeing her curiously.

She grasped a thread of the net and tugged. The web of knotted string fell apart and shrank, leaving her holding only a piece of twine. She tucked that into her pocket and wound the free end of the dragon's leash around her wrist.

My father and the others had left the safety of the trees and were advancing warily. Lindri waited for them, rocking on her heels as the dragon butted her affectionately with its head.

"You tricked us!" Halen screeched when he was close enough that she could hear. "You never told us—" He couldn't seem to remember what she hadn't told them. His face turned mottled purple as he opened and closed his mouth soundlessly.

"You didn't believe me when I told you something about their habits," Lindri said calmly as she rubbed the dragon's muzzle. The elders stopped twenty feet away from her, refusing to draw closer. "Would you have believed me if I told you about this?"

When they didn't answer, she led the dragon to her cart and hitched it at the back. The gelding looked at the lizard in a bored way, as if dragons always brought up the rear.

Perhaps dragons always did.

"What will you do with it now?" My father sounded nervous. I looked away from him. Any love I felt for him had gone in the night, but I hated to see him trying to be humble to her now. "We meant you no harm—"

Lindri climbed onto the driver's seat of her cart and picked up the reins. "He's lost," she said briefly. "I'm taking him home to his mountains."

"*Lost?*" Halen whispered.

"He would never have come this far if he hadn't been lost in the first place." Her mouth curled scornfully. "Neither would he have done so much damage if folk like you hadn't insisted on feeding him their children." She looked down at me. "Why don't you come with me, Tonya? I'll take you someplace where you can get a proper magical education."

I seized the edge of her seat. "I don't want to learn someplace else," I told her. "I want to study with you. I want to learn what *you* can teach me."

Lindri raised her brows, her gray eyes puzzled. "This? It's just plain magic, Tonya. Nothing spectacular."

I glanced at the dragon following the cart, attached only by what had once been a piece of string. He—she had said it was a he—nibbled curiously at the wooden step under the rear door. "It's spectacular enough," I told her.

Lindri laughed. Suddenly I could see she wasn't old at all—she was barely a handful more of years older than I. "Come up, then," she said, offering her hand. "What I have to teach you, I will." ❧

The Bureau
d'Echange de Maux

Lord Dunsany

I often think of the Bureau d'Echange de Maux and the won-
drously evil old man that sat therein. It stood in a little street
that there is in Paris, its doorway made of three brown beams of wood,
the top one overlapping the others like the Greek letter pi, all the rest
painted green, a house far lower and narrower than its neighbours and
infinitely stranger, a thing to take one's fancy. And over the doorway on
the old brown beam in faded yellow letters this legend ran, 'Bureau
Universel d'Echange de Maux.'[1]

I entered at once and accosted the listless man that lolled on a stool
by his counter. I demanded the wherefore of his wonderful house, what
evil wares he exchanged, with many other things that I wished to know,
for curiosity led me: and indeed had it not I had gone at once from the
shop, for there was so evil a look in that fattened man, in the hang of his
fallen cheeks and his sinful eye, that you would have said he had had
dealings with Hell and won the advantage by sheer wickedness.

Such a man was mine host, but above all the evil of him lay in his eyes,
which lay so still, so apathetic, that you would have sworn that he was
drugged or dead; like lizards motionless on a wall they lay, then suddenly
they darted, and all his cunning flamed up and revealed itself in what
one moment before seemed no more than a sleepy and ordinary wicked

1 **Bureau Universel d'Echange de Maux:** French for Universal Office for the
Exchange of Evils

old man. And this was the object and trade of that peculiar shop, the Bureau Universel d'Echange de Maux: you paid twenty francs, which the old man proceeded to take from me, for admission to the bureau, and then had the right to exchange any evil or misfortune with anyone on the premises for some evil or misfortune that he 'could afford,' as the old man put it.

There were four or five men in the dingy ends of that low-ceilinged room who gesticulated[2] and muttered softly in twos as men who make a bargain, and now and then more came in, and the eyes of the flabby owner of the house leaped up at them as they entered, seemed to know their errands at once and each one's peculiar need, and fell back again into somnolence,[3] receiving his twenty francs in an almost lifeless hand and biting the coin as though in pure absence of mind.

'Some of my clients,' he told me. So amazing to me was the trade of this extraordinary shop that I engaged the old man in conversation, repulsive though he was, and from his garrulity[4] I gathered these facts. He spoke in perfect English though his utterance was somewhat thick and heavy, no language seemed to come amiss[5] to him. He had been in business a great many years, how many he would not say, and was far older than he looked. All kinds of people did business in his shop. What they exchanged with each other he did not care, except that it had to be evils; he was not empowered to carry on any other kind of business.

There was no evil, he told me, that was not negotiable[6] there; no evil the old man knew had ever been taken away in despair from his shop. A man might have to wait and come back again next day and next day and the day after, paying twenty francs each time, but the old man had the addresses of his clients and shrewdly knew their needs, and soon the right two met and eagerly changed their commodities.[7] 'Commodities' was the old man's terrible word, said with a gruesome smack of his heavy lips, for he took a pride in his business and evils to him were goods.

I learned from him in ten minutes very much of human nature, more than I had ever learned from any other man; I learned from him

2 **gesticulated:** to make gestures while speaking

3 **somnolence:** drowsiness; sleepiness

4 **garrulity:** quality of giving rambling and pointless speeches

5 **amiss:** incorrectly

6 **negotiable:** up for trade

7 **commodities:** items for sale or trade

that a man's own evil is to him the worst thing that there is or could be, and that an evil so unbalances all men's minds that they always seek for extremes in that small grim shop. A woman that had no children had exchanged with an impoverished half-maddened creature with twelve. On one occasion a man had exchanged wisdom for folly.

'Why on earth did he do that?' I said.

'None of my business,' the old man answered in his heavy indolent[8] way. He merely took his twenty francs from each and ratified[9] the agreement in the little room at the back opening out of the shop where his clients do business. Apparently the man that had parted with wisdom had left the shop upon the tips of his toes with a happy though foolish expression all over his face, but the other went thoughtfully away wearing a troubled and very puzzled look. Almost always it seemed they did business in opposite evils.

But the thing that puzzled me most in all my talks with that unwieldy man, the thing that puzzles me still, is that none that had once done business in that shop ever returned again; a man might come day after day for many weeks, but once do business and he never returned; so much the old man told me, but, when I asked him why, he only muttered that he did not know.

It was to discover the wherefore of this strange thing, and for no other reason at all, that I determined myself to do business sooner or later in the little room at the back of that mysterious shop. I determined to exchange some very trivial evil for some evil equally slight, to seek for myself an advantage so very small as scarcely to give Fate as it were a grip; for I deeply distrusted these bargains, knowing well that man has never yet benefited by the marvellous and that the more miraculous his

8 **indolent:** sluggish; lazy

9 **ratified:** approved; made legal

advantage appears to be the more securely and tightly do the gods or the witches catch him. In a few days more I was going back to England and I was beginning to fear that I should be sea-sick: this fear of sea-sickness, not the actual malady but only the mere fear of it, I decided to exchange for a suitably little evil. I did not know with whom I should be dealing, who in reality was the head of the firm (one never does when shopping), but I decided that no one could make very much on so small a bargain as that.

I told the old man my project, and he scoffed at the smallness of my commodity, trying to urge me on to some darker bargain, but could not move me from my purpose. And then he told me tales with a somewhat boastful air of the big business, the great bargains, that had passed through his hands. A man had once run in there to try to exchange death; he had swallowed poison by accident and had only twelve hours to live. That sinister old man had been able to oblige him. A client was willing to exchange the commodity.

'But what did he give in exchange for death?' I said.

'Life,' said that grim old man with a furtive chuckle.

'It must have been a horrible life,' I said.

'That was not my affair,' the proprietor said, lazily rattling together as he spoke a little pocketful of twenty-franc pieces.

Strange business I watched in that shop for the next few days, the exchange of odd commodities, and heard strange mutterings in corners amongst couples who presently rose and went to the back room, the old man following to ratify.

Twice a day for a week I paid my twenty francs, watching life with its great needs and its little needs morning and afternoon spread out before me in all its wonderful variety.

And one day I met a comfortable man with only a little need, he seemed to have the very evil I wanted. He always feared the lift was going to break. I knew too much of hydraulics to fear things as silly as that, but it was not my business to cure his ridiculous fear. Very few words were needed to convince him that mine was the evil for him, he never crossed the sea, and I, on the other hand, could always walk upstairs, and I also felt at the time, as many must feel in that shop, that so absurd a fear could never trouble me. And yet at times it is almost the curse of my life. When we both had signed the parchment in the spidery back room and the old man had signed and ratified (for which we had to pay him fifty francs each) I went back to my hotel, and there I saw the deadly thing in the basement. They asked me if I would go upstairs in the lift; from force of habit I risked it, and I held my breath all the way up and clenched my hands. Nothing will induce me to try such a journey again. I would sooner go up to my room in a balloon. And why? Because if a balloon goes wrong you have a chance, it may spread out into a parachute after it has burst, it may catch in a tree, a hundred and one things may happen, but if a lift falls down its shaft you are done. As for sea-sickness I shall never be sick again, I cannot tell you why except that I know that it is so.

And the shop in which I made this remarkable bargain, the shop to which none return when their business is done: I set out for it next day. Blindfold I could have found my way to the unfashionable quarter out of which a mean street runs, where you take the alley at the end, whence runs the cul-de-sac[10] where the queer shop stood. A shop with pillars, fluted and painted red, stands on its near side, its other neighbour is a low-class jeweller's with little silver brooches in the window. In such incongruous company stood the shop with beams, with its walls painted green.

In half an hour I stood in the cul-de-sac to which I had gone twice a day for the last week. I found the shop with the ugly painted pillars and the jeweller that sold brooches, but the green house with the three beams was gone.

Pulled down, you will say, although in a single night. That can never be the answer to the mystery, for the house of the fluted pillars painted on plaster, and the low-class jeweller's shop with its silver brooches (all of which I could identify one by one) were standing side by side. ∾

---

10 **cul-de-sac:** a street or alley closed at one end

Ms. Lipshutz
and the Goblin

Marvin Kaye

*L*ipshutz, Daphne A., Ms. (age: 28; height: 5' 2"; weight: 160 lbs.; must wear corrective lenses), had frizzy brown hair, buck teeth, and an almost terminal case of acne. Though her mother frequently reassured her she had a Very Nice Personality, that commodity seemed of little value in Daphne's Quest for The Perfect Mate.

According to Daphne A. (for Arabella) Lipshutz, The Perfect Mate must be 30, about 5' 9" in height, weigh approximately 130 pounds, have wavy blond hair (1st preference), white teeth, a gentle smile and peaches-and-cream complexion.

Daphne's Quest for The Perfect Mate was hampered by her job as an interviewer (2nd grade) for the State of New York, Manhattan division of the Labor Department's Upper West Side office of the Bureau of Unemployment. The only men she met there were sour-stomached married colleagues, or the people she processed for unemployment checks, "and them," her mother cautioned, "you can do without. Who'd buy the tickets, tip the cabbie, shmeer[1] the headwaiter, pick up the check?"

Ms. Lipshutz worked in a dingy green office around the corner from a supermarket. To get there, she had to take a southbound bus from The Bronx, get off at 90th and Broadway and walk west past a narrow, dark alley. Next to it was a brick building with a doorway providing access to steep wooden stairs that mounted[2] to her office. The stairs were worn

---

1 **shmeer:** bribe
2 **mounted:** led upward

smooth and low in the middle of each step by innumerable shuffling feet. Daphne noticed that unemployed feet frequently shuffle.

Late one October afternoon, just before Hallowe'en, Ms. Lipshutz was about to take her final coffee-break of the day when an unusual personage entered the unemployment bureau and approached her window. He was six feet eight inches tall and thin as a breadstick. There were warts all over his body, and the color of his skin was bright green.

Ms. Lipshutz thought he looked like the Jolly Green Pickle or an elongated cousin of Peter Pan. He was certainly the ugliest thing she'd ever set her soulful brown eyes on.

Leaning his pointy elbows on her window-shelf, the newcomer glanced admiringly at her acne-dimpled face and asked whether he was in the correct line. He addressed her as Miss.

Bridling,[3] Daphne told him to address her as *Ms.* The tall green creature's eyebrows rose.

"Miz?" he echoed, mystified. "What dat?"

"I am a liberated woman," she said in the clockwork rhythm of a civil servant or a missioned spirit. Her vocal timbre was flat and nasal, pure Grand Concourse.[4] "I do not like to be called Miss. If I were married—" (here she betrayed her cause with a profound sigh) "—I would not call myself Mrs. So please call me Ms."

The green one nodded. "Me once had girlfriend named Miz. Shlubya Miz. She great big troll. You troll?"

"This," said Ms. Lipshutz, "is an immaterial conversation. Please state your name and business."

"Name: Klotsch."

"Would you repeat that?" she asked, fishing out an application form and poising a pencil.

"Klotsch."

"First or last?"

"Always!"

Unusual names were common at the unemployment office, and so was unusual stupidity. Ms. Lipshutz patiently explained she wanted to know whether Klotsch was a first or last name.

"Only name. Just Klotsch."

---

3 **bridling:** getting mildly angry
4 **Grand Concourse:** flat nasal accent common to the Grand Concourse area of the Bronx

"How do you spell it? Is that C as in Couch?"

"K as in Kill!" Klotsch shouted. "Kill-LOTSCH!"

"Kindly lower your voice," she said mechanically. "I presume you wish to apply for unemployment checks?"

Spreading his warty hands, the big green thing grinned. "Klotsch not come to count your pimples, Miz."

Not realizing the remark was meant flirtatiously, Daphne, who was extremely sensitive about her acne, took offense. "That was a cruel thing to say!"

"How come?" Klotsch was puzzled.

"Me no understand. Klotsch like pimples. You lots cuter than Shlubya the troll!"

Daphne, not very reassured, found it wise to retreat into the prescribed formulae[5] of the State of New York for dealing with an unemployment insurance applicant.

"Now," she began. "Mister Klotsch—"

He waved a deprecatory[6] claw. "No Mister."

"I beg your pardon?"

"You liberated, so okay, Klotsch liberated, too. If you Miz, me *Murr*."

"I see," she said primly, unable to determine whether she was being made fun of. Inscribing Klotsch's name on Form NYS204-A, Ms. Lipshutz requested his address.

"Not got."

"You are a transient?"[7]

He shook his shaggy head. "Me are a goblin."

"No, no, Murr Klotsch, we are not up to Employment History yet. Simply state your address."

"Me don't got. Landlady kick me out of cave."

"Oh, dear. Couldn't you pay your rent?"

"Ate landlord," Klotsch glumly confessed.

Daphne suddenly noticed that Klotsch had two lower incisors which protruded three inches north of his upper lip. Civic conscience aroused, she told him eating his landlord was a terrible thing to do.

"Telling me! Klotsch sick three days."

"Do you go round eating people all the time?"

---

5 **prescribed formulae:** proper procedure

6 **deprecatory:** disapproving; offended

7 **transient:** person without a permanent home or dwelling

The goblin drew himself erect, his pride hurt. "Klotsch no eat people! Only landlords!"

Ms. Lipshutz conceded the distinction. Returning to the form, she asked Klotsch for his last date of employment.

He sighed gloomily. "October 31st, 1877."

Time to be firm: "The unemployment relief act, Murr Klotsch, does *not* cover cases prior to 1932."

"So put down 1932," he suggested. In an uncharacteristic spirit of compromise, Daphne promptly complied. (It was eight minutes before five o'clock.)

"Place of previous employment?"

"Black Forest."

"Is that in New York?"

"Is Germany."

"You may not be aware that the State of New York does not share reciprocity[8] with overseas powers."

Klotsch thought about it briefly, then raised a crooked talon in recollection. "Once did one-night gig in Poughkeepsie."

"Check." She wrote it down. "Previous employer's name."

"Beelzebub."[9]

Ms. Lipshutz stuck pencil and application in Klotsch's paws. "Here— *you* tackle that one!" While he wrote, she studied him, deciding that, after all, Klotsch wasn't *so* bad looking. He had a kind of sexy expression in his big purple eye.

"And where does this Mist—uh, Murr Beelzebub conduct his business?"

The goblin shrugged. "Usually hangs around Times Square."

"Then he does not maintain a permanent place of business?"

"Oh, yeah: further south." Klotsch shook his large head, scowling. "He no good boss, got all goblins unionized. Me no like. Klotsch work for self."

Ms. Lipshutz muttered something about scabs. Klotsch, misunderstanding, beamed toothily. "Klotsch got plenty scabs. You like?"

Eye on the clock (four of five), Ms. Lipshutz proceeded with her routine. "Have you received any recent employment offers?"

"Just Beelzebub."

8 **reciprocity:** recognition by one country of another country's laws and privileges

9 **Beelzebub:** the devil

"Do you mean," she inquired with the frosty, lofty disapproval of an accredited representative of the State of New York, "that you have refused a job offer?"

"Me no going to shovel coal!" Klotsch howled, eyes glowing like the embers he disdained.

Ms. Lipshutz understood. "So long as the position was not in your chosen professional line." She ticked off another question on the form. "That brings us, Murr Klotsch, to the kind of work you are seeking. What precisely do you do?"

He replied in a solemn guttural tone. "Me goblin."

"What does that entail?"

By way of demonstration, Klotsch uttered a fearful yell, gnashed his teeth and dashed up and down the walls. He panted, snorted, whistled, screamed, swung from the light fixtures and dripped green on various desks. Ms. Lipshutz's colleagues paid no attention. Worse things happen in Manhattan.

Gibbering his last gibber, Klotsch returned to Ms. Lipshutz's window. "That my Class A material. You like?"

"Interesting," she conceded. "Did you get much call for that sort of thing?"

"Plenty work once! Double-time during day! Klotsch used to frighten farmers, shepherds, even once in a while, genuine hero." He sighed, shrugging eloquently. "But then scare biz go down toilet. They bust me down to kids, then not even them. Too many other scary things nowadays, goblins outclassed."

She nodded, not without hasty sympathy (two of five). "And have you ever considered changing your profession?"

"Got plenty monsters already on TV, movies, comics."

"What about the armed services?"

Klotsch shook his big green head. "All the best jobs already got by trolls."

Ms. Lipshutz sighed. She would have liked to assist Klotsch, but it was 4:59 and she did not want to miss the 5:03 bus. Setting his form aside for processing the following day, she asked him to return in one week.

The hapless goblin shambled out without another word.

▲   ▲   ▲

Ms. Lipshutz hurried on her coat and hat, locked up her desk, pattered swiftly down the old stairs to catch the 5:03.

Turning east, she heel-clicked toward Broadway. There was a dark alleyway separating the corner supermarket from the building that housed the unemployment bureau. As she passed it, a great green goblin leaped out at her, whoofling, snorting and howling in outrageous menace.

Daphne nearly collapsed with laughter. She snickered, tittered, chortled and giggled for nearly a minute before gaining sufficient self-control to speak. "Murr Klotsch . . . it's you!"

His face was sad and long. "Miz no scared, she laugh."

"Oh . . . oh, *no!*" Daphne consolingly reached out her hand and touched him. "Murr Klotsch . . . I was so, *so* frightened!"

"Then why you laugh?"

"I was positively . . . uh . . . hysterical with fear!"

The goblin grinned shyly, hopefully. "No kidding?"

"Truly," she declared firmly, coyly adding, "I don't believe my heart will stop pounding until I've had a drink."

So she missed the 5:03 and Klotsch took her to a nearby Chinese restaurant where the bartender mixed excellent zombies.[10] Just as her mother always warned, Daphne was stuck paying the bar bill. But somehow, she didn't mind.

▲   ▲   ▲

Ms. Daphne Arabella Lipshutz (age: 28 1/2; weight: 110 lbs., wears contact lenses) wedded Klotsch the following spring despite her mother's protests that she surely could have found a nice Jewish goblin somewhere.

"And what about the children?" she shrilled. "Suppose they resemble their father?"

---

10 **zombies:** mixed drinks made of rum and fruit juice

Daphne shrugged. "He's not bad once you get used to him."

With the combined aid of his wife and the New York State Department of Labor, Klotsch found work in an amusement park fun house, where he made such a hit that a talent scout caught his act and signed him up. Since then, the goblin has made several horror films, appears on TV talk shows (as guest host on one of them), endorses a brand of green toothpaste and is part owner of a line of Hallowe'en masks. The couple moved to the suburbs, where Mrs. Lipshutz often visits her illustrious son-in-law.

The only unfortunate result of their marriage is that it has worked wonders with Daphne's complexion. But Klotsch is too considerate to mention his disappointment. ❧

The Chaser

John Collier

$\mathcal{A}$lan Austen, as nervous as a kitten, went up certain dark and creaky stairs in the neighborhood of Pell Street, and peered about for a long time on the dim landing before he found the name he wanted written obscurely on one of the doors.

He pushed open this door, as he had been told to do, and found himself in a tiny room, which contained no furniture but a plain kitchen table, a rocking-chair, and an ordinary chair. On one of the dirty buff-colored walls were a couple of shelves, containing in all perhaps a dozen bottles and jars.

An old man sat in the rocking-chair, reading a newspaper. Alan, without a word, handed him the card he had been given. "Sit down, Mr. Austen," said the old man very politely. "I am glad to make your acquaintance."

"Is it true," asked Alan, "that you have a certain mixture that has—er—quite extraordinary effects?"

"My dear sir," replied the old man, "my stock in trade is not very large—I don't deal in laxatives and teething mixtures—but such as it is, it is varied. I think nothing I sell has effects which could be precisely described as ordinary."

"Well, the fact is—" began Alan.

"Here, for example," interrupted the old man, reaching for a bottle from the shelf. "Here is a liquid as colorless as water, almost tasteless, quite imperceptible[1] in coffee, milk, wine, or any other beverage. It is also quite imperceptible to any known method of autopsy."

"Do you mean it is a poison?" cried Alan, very much horrified.

"Call it a glove-cleaner if you like," said the old man indifferently. "Maybe it will clean gloves. I have never tried. One might call it a life-cleaner. Lives need cleaning sometimes."

"I want nothing of that sort," said Alan.

"Probably it is just as well," said the old man. "Do you know the price of this? For one teaspoonful, which is sufficient, I ask five thousand dollars. Never less. Not a penny less."

"I hope all your mixtures are not as expensive," said Alan apprehensively.

"Oh dear, no," said the old man. "It would be no good charging that sort of price for a love potion, for example. Young people who need a love potion very seldom have five thousand dollars. Otherwise they would not need a love potion."

"I am glad to hear that," said Alan.

"I look at it like this," said the old man. "Please a customer with one article, and he will come back when he needs another. Even if it *is* more costly. He will save up for it, if necessary."

"So," said Alan, "you really do sell love potions?"

"If I did not sell love potions," said the old man, reaching for another bottle, "I should not have mentioned the other matter to you. It is only when one is in a position to oblige that one can afford to be so confidential."[2]

"And these potions," said Alan. "They are not just—just—er—"

"Oh, no," said the old man. "Their effects are permanent, and extend far beyond casual impulse. But they include it. Bountifully, insistently. Everlastingly."

1 **imperceptible:** not noticeable
2 **confidential:** willing to share

"Dear me!" said Alan, attempting a look of scientific detachment. "How very interesting!"

"But consider the spiritual side," said the old man.

"I do, indeed," said Alan.

"For indifference," said the old man, "they substitute devotion. For scorn, adoration. Give one tiny measure of this to the young lady—its flavor is imperceptible in orange juice, soup, or cocktails—and however gay and giddy she is, she will change altogether. She will want nothing but solitude, and you."

"I can hardly believe it," said Alan. "She is so fond of parties."

"She will not like them anymore," said the old man. "She will be afraid of the pretty girls you may meet."

"She will actually be jealous?" cried Alan in a rapture. "Of me?"

"Yes, she will want to be everything to you."

"She is, already. Only she doesn't care about it."

"She will, when she has taken this. She will care intensely. You will be her sole interest in life."

"Wonderful!" cried Alan.

"She will want to know all you do," said the old man. "All that has happened to you during the day. Every word of it. She will want to know what you are thinking about, why you smile suddenly, why you are looking sad."

"That is love!" cried Alan.

"Yes," said the old man. "How carefully she will look after you! She will never allow you to be tired, to sit in a draught, to neglect your food. If you are an hour late, she will be terrified. She will think you are killed, or that some siren[3] has caught you."

"I can hardly imagine Diana like that!" cried Alan, overwhelmed with joy.

"You will not have to use your imagination," said the old man. "And, by the way, since there are always sirens, if by any chance you *should*, later on, slip a little, you need not worry. She will forgive you, in the end. She will be terribly hurt, of course, but she will forgive you—in the end."

"That will not happen," said Alan fervently.

---

3 **siren:** one of a group of women in Greek mythology who lure sailors to destruction by their singing; temptress

"Of course not," said the old man. "But, if it did, you need not worry. She would never divorce you. Oh, no! And, of course, she herself will never give you the least, the very least, grounds for—uneasiness."

"And how much," said Alan, "is this wonderful mixture?"

"It is not as dear," said the old man, "as the glove-cleaner, or life-cleaner, as I sometimes call it. No. That is five thousand dollars, never a penny less. One has to be older than you are, to indulge in that sort of thing. One has to save up for it."

"But the love potion?" said Alan.

"Oh, that," said the old man, opening the drawer in the kitchen table, and taking out a tiny, rather dirty-looking phial.[4] "That is just a dollar."

"I can't tell you how grateful I am," said Alan, watching him fill it.

"I like to oblige," said the old man. "Then customers come back, later in life, when they are rather better off, and want more expensive things. Here you are. You will find it very effective."

"Thank you again," said Alan. "Good-by."

"*Au revoir*,"[5] said the old man. ∞

---

4 **phial:** a small jar

5 *au revoir*: French for "good-bye"; literally it means "til we see each other again."

Responding to Cluster Two

What Can Fantasy Teach Us?
Thinking Skill ANALYZING

1. Why do you think Lindri calls her abilities "just plain magic. . . . Nothing spectacular"?

2. **Satire** pokes fun at human weaknesses, ideas, customs, and institutions. In your opinion, what things are being satirized in "Ms. Lipshutz and the Goblin"?

3. In "The Chaser" why do you think the love potion is only a dollar while the "life-cleanser" costs thousands?

4. Add the selections in this cluster to the fantasy classification chart you began at the end of Cluster One.

5. Using **analysis**, decide what lesson is taught by each story in this cluster.

Writing Activity: The Moral of the Story
The stories in this cluster use fantasy to teach lessons or morals. Choose a proverb from those below or think up your own. Then create an outline for a fantasy story that could teach this lesson. You may want to refer to the analysis you did in Question 5 above for ideas. For fun, read your outline to your classmates without sharing the proverb it is based on. See if they can guess the proverb.

You can't teach an old dog new tricks   *Beauty is only skin deep*

A fool and his money are soon parted   *Two heads are better than one*

People in glass houses shouldn't throw stones   *Children should be seen not heard*

Your Story Outline Should Include
• story setting
• main characters in story
• problem or conflict the story needs to resolve
• main events in plot
• solution or conclusion
• lesson or moral (proverb used as basis for story)

CLUSTER THREE

What's Real and How Do You Know?
Thinking Skill EVALUATING

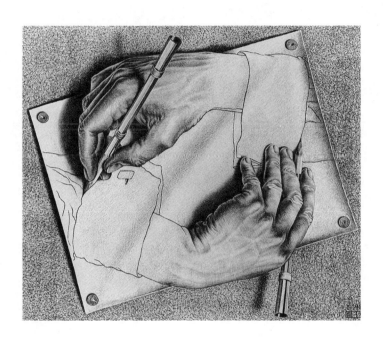

Frances Griffiths with fairy, photographed by Elsie Wright, 1920

"Ticing" the Fairies

Wim Coleman

In 1917, the most terrible war humanity had ever endured was raging for its third year. It was called the Great War—or sometimes the World War, because so much of the world was fighting. In the same year, ten-year-old Frances Griffiths arrived in Cottingley, a village in Yorkshire, England. Frances had lived most of her life in South Africa. When her father joined the fighting, Frances went on an extended visit to relatives in Cottingley.

Frances and her sixteen-year-old cousin Elsie Wright began to spend long afternoons playing by the nearby "beck," a Yorkshire word for a creek or stream. To her delight, Frances saw many fairies there. She had never seen fairies back in South Africa. ("It must be too hot for them there," she wrote home to a friend.)

One afternoon in July while enticing the fairies—or "ticing" them, as she liked to say—Frances fell in the beck and got her clothes wet. She got a scolding from Polly and Arthur Wright, her aunt and uncle. Arthur, a no-nonsense fellow, was angered by Frances' insistence that the episode had been caused by fairies. Poor Frances was reduced to tears.

Elsie was very upset by her parents' unfairness toward her cousin. So she asked her father if she and Frances could borrow his camera for a while. Surely, she thought, her parents would be convinced by photographs of fairies.

Now, many skeptics will object to this version of how the Cottingley case began. They will insist that Frances and Elsie never saw fairies at all. But two girls seeing fairies in Yorkshire seems sanity itself when compared to the madness running rampant elsewhere in the world at the time.

Arthur reluctantly lent Elsie his camera. It was called a "Midg," and it used glass plates instead of rolls of film. It was fairly crude, not known for getting sharp images. But Elsie and Frances took it eagerly to the beck that sunny, Saturday afternoon. A half hour later, they rushed excitedly back to the house, insisting that Arthur immediately develop the picture. Arthur went to his darkroom and set warily to work.

The image that appeared was far from clear—but then, Elsie had never taken a photograph before. In the center of the rectangular frame was Frances' face, slightly out of focus, staring dreamily (or was it boredly?) into the camera. Behind Frances to her right was a lovely waterfall. Her elbows were planted on a mossy mound, upon which were four small, vague white figures. Elsie and Frances said that these were dancing fairies.

Arthur didn't believe it, nor did his wife, Polly. But he lent the girls the camera again on another sunny day in August. They took it to the beck and returned as excited as before. This time, Frances had taken the photograph. It showed Elsie sitting on the grass, extending her hand to a twelve-inch tall winged figure. Frances and Elsie claimed the little creature was a gnome—a kind of dwarf familiar in fairy tales.

Arthur was sure that the girls were playing a joke—for they really did love a joke. Moreover, they were wasting expensive photographic plates, so he never lent them the Midg again. The girls weren't especially heartbroken. As for the two photographs, they passed them around to friends and relatives who didn't know what to make of them.

The Great War ended in November 1918. By then, Frances' father had returned safely from France. Instead of going back to South Africa, Frances and her family resettled in the English coastal city of Scarborough, not very far from Cottingley. So Frances was able to visit her cousin often, and the two continued to "tice" the fairies by the beck—not that anyone really cared. For awhile, it seemed as if the fairy photographs would be forgotten, even by the girls themselves.

But Frances and Elsie were not the only members of the family with a mystical turn of mind. Although Polly Wright didn't put much stock in the fairy photographs, she had strange experiences of her own, including astral projections (in which one's conscious self leaves one's body) and memories of past lives. Arthur, of course, had no sympathy for this kind of thing, but Polly found fellowship in the Theosophical Society.

This mystical organization, which still exists today, was very influential in England and America during the early years of the twentieth century. Theosophy combines the ideas of Eastern religions such as Hinduism and Buddhism with a belief in extraordinary phenomena, including clairvoyance (the ability to perceive objects outside one's field of vision) and mediumship (the ability to communicate with the spirits of the dead).

In 1919, Polly Wright attended a Theosophical Society meeting at which the lecture topic was fairies. Not surprisingly, Theosophical doctrine took a stand in favor of their existence. Was it possible, Polly now wondered, that Elsie and Frances really saw fairies by the beck—and that the photographs they had taken three years earlier were genuine?

Polly told the lecturer about the photographs, then later sent him prints. In the early months of 1920, the prints reached Edward Gardner, an influential Theosophist, who had them professionally sharpened. The figures in front of Frances were clearly fairies, three of them with wings. And the creature in the second photograph was unmistakably a gnome. (Of course, the airbrushed "sharpening" of the photographs proved quite controversial.)

Gardner sent prints of the pictures to his friend, the famous author Sir Arthur Conan Doyle. Doyle is best known as the creator of the celebrated fictional detective Sherlock Holmes, a hard-headed rationalist who, in at least one story, declared his disbelief in the supernatural. But the author's ideas were not the same as those of his character, for Doyle was an outspoken proponent of Spiritualism. Like Theosophy, Spiritualism emphasized the supernatural, especially communications with the dead.

Theosophy and Spiritualism were only two of many such movements in the early twentieth century. Why was there so much interest in mysticism then? The nineteenth century had brought great intellectual and technological changes—including the coining of the word "scientist" in 1840. The secrets of electricity had been unlocked, and by the turn of the century public use of electrical power was widespread. Before the beginning of the World War, automobiles were also common, and powered flight was a reality.

Such developments were beneficial in many ways, but they also had a darker side, which became evident during the war. No sooner had humankind conquered the air than aviators began bombing cities. Terrible new weapons included tanks, machine guns, and poison gas. War began threatening even civilian populations in frightful new ways.

But most disturbingly to many people, religion seemed undermined by scientific discoveries. In 1859, Charles Darwin published *Origin of Species*, which argued that all living creatures—including human beings—evolved from a common ancestor. Darwin's theories seemed to make a creator deity completely unnecessary. People were stunned by Darwin's book. The age of scientific materialism was underway; could faith survive?

The Great War seemed an awful climax to a long spiritual crisis. Its carnage was blamed as much on scientific materialism as on runaway technology. Civilization itself appeared to have lost its spiritual bearings, and human life no longer had its once sacred value. It seems small wonder that so many people took refuge in mysticism.

Doyle was personally affected by the tragedy of the war. In 1918, his son Kingsley died as a result of injuries he had suffered at the Battle of Somme in 1916. Doyle did not have the comfort of religion to help him through this loss, for his faith had been shattered by reading Darwin. Even before Kingsley's death, Doyle had flirted with Spiritualism. Might it restore civilization's waning sense of the sacred—on a fully scientific basis?

Perhaps understandably, Doyle's grief for Kingsley made him a full convert to Spiritualism. In 1925, he even claimed to have heard Kingsley speak to him during a seance—a session in which a medium summons the spirits of the dead.

It makes sense, then, that Doyle was convinced by the photographs. He published them along with an article he wrote about fairies for the 1920 Christmas issue of *Strand Magazine*, the periodical in which most of the Sherlock Holmes stories first appeared. Doyle's article told how the photographs had been taken by two girls in Yorkshire—although, to protect their privacy, he renamed them "Alice" and "Iris."

With his Holmes-like eye, Doyle pointed out many striking details in the photographs. For example, the fairies in the first picture were playing pipes. And in the second picture, he saw a spot on the gnome's belly which he concluded was a navel. To Doyle, this proved that gnomes reproduced in much the same manner as human beings.

Doyle's article and the published photographs created a sensation. For many people, the photographs were undeniable proof of the existence of fairies, but others raised nagging questions. Why, for example, did some of the fairies sport contemporary clothes and hairstyles? Since when had fairies been fashion-conscious?

Frances Griffiths, 1917

Gardner and Doyle had no trouble with questions. The fairies, they believed, were made of a mysterious substance called ectoplasm which flowed from the girls' minds. While the fairies were certainly real, their shapes were influenced by the girls' concepts of fairies. And "Alice" and "Iris" would naturally visualize modern-looking fairies.

"Alice" and "Iris" did not remain anonymous for long. A reporter uncovered their identities and went to Yorkshire to interview the Wrights. To the family's dismay, more reporters followed. There was little hope that the fairy pictures would soon be forgotten.

To the contrary, Doyle and Gardner wanted more pictures, and even before the publication of the *Strand* article, Gardner went to Cottingley to get them. Since Arthur Wright had forbidden Elsie and Frances to use his Midg, Gardner took two cameras.

Gardner was undismayed when Frances and Elsie told him that he could not accompany them to the beck. After all, fairies were known to be shy, and they were unlikely to appear except in the presence of kindred spirits—especially children. (With typical Victorian chauvinism, Gardner seems to have regarded Elsie, then nineteen, as a child.) He left the cameras with the cousins, returned to London, and waited.

His wait was not in vain. During the spring of 1921, Elsie and Frances took three more pictures. The first showed a startled Frances with a fairy leaping before her nose. The second showed another airborne fairy offering flowers to Elsie. The last photograph was harder to make out, but Doyle said it showed sunbathing fairies awakening from a nap.

In 1921, Doyle published another *Strand* article featuring the new photographs. Like the first article, this one stirred up a storm of controversy. All England was caught up in fairy fever—except Frances and Elsie, for in 1921, they stopped seeing fairies altogether. Elsie was quite grown up by then, and although Frances was only fourteen, she was serious and scholarly and too mature for such childish interests.

Soon, Frances and Elsie quietly slipped out of the public eye—at least for a time. Both women married and became mothers and grandmothers. The fairies stopped playing any significant part in their lives. But for many other people, the fascination continued. Sir Arthur Conan Doyle lived until 1930, writing and lecturing about Spiritualism and the fairies until he died. He never questioned the photographs' authenticity.

Years passed, and the photographs were never forgotten. But little by little, doubters asked increasingly damaging questions. They pointed out that Elsie had always been a skillful artist and had done a short stint as a photographer's assistant. Might she have used her drawing skills and her knowledge of photography to fake the pictures?

Doubters also pointed out that the dancing fairies in the first photograph looked uncannily like an illustration in *Princess Mary's Gift Book*, published in 1915. (Ironically, Doyle never noticed this resemblance, despite the fact that a story of his own appeared in the same book.) It seemed likely that the first photograph was based on this illustration.

Eventually, reporters sought out the cousins again. In 1981, eighty-year-old Elsie finally confessed, and in 1982 Frances followed suit. The fairies, they explained, were simply drawings cut out of poster board. Elsie had, indeed, traced the fairies in the first photograph from *Princess Mary's Gift Book*.

The cutouts had been propped or perched on hat pins. The fairies and the gnome in the first two photographs were stuck in the ground and photographed with Frances and Elsie. What Doyle had thought was the gnome's navel was really just a hat pin. The flying fairies in the third and fourth photographs had been pinned to tree branches.

And so the case of the Cottingley fairies was closed. But oddly enough, the fairies became more popular than ever. People have been talking and writing about them incessantly ever since. And in 1997, two films inspired by the Cottingley fairies appeared—*Fairy Tale: A True Story* and *Photographing Fairies*.

So the mystery of the Cottingley fairies still fascinates, perhaps because unanswered questions lurk just beneath the story's surface. Even in their old age, Frances and Elsie insisted that they really saw fairies as children. So in just what sense were the photographs faked? Isn't it possible, at the start, that Elsie truly wanted to depict what she and her cousin thought they had seen? No doubt, a prankish desire to puncture adult self-certainty played an important role. But was it really full-blown fraud at the beginning?

Of course, Elsie and Frances both admitted to a hoax, but when did it really *become* a hoax? Was it when they took that first picture—or the second, third, fourth, or fifth? Or was it only when they remembered the episode in the self-certainty of their own adulthood?

Debunkers will insist that such questions are beside the point, but debunkers didn't fare well in the Cottingley case. In 1920, experts at Kodak suspected the work of a professional photographer. Around the same time, psychical researcher Sir Oliver Lodge suggested that the first picture was staged with dancers. And during the 1970s, the famous debunker James "The Amazing" Randi analyzed the photographs and thought he saw *strings* holding up the fairies. Even debunkers sometimes imagine things.

The last photograph—the one that Doyle thought showed fairies awakening from a nap—remains puzzling. Elsie eventually claimed that it was also a fake, and that she took it herself. But Frances always insisted that it was the only authentic photograph of the five—and that *she* took it herself! Why the conflicting stories?

Photographic experts believe that the last picture is the only double exposure of the five. In all likelihood, Elsie took one exposure of cutout fairies on the grass. Then, not knowing that her cousin had already exposed the negative, Frances snapped another shot, accidentally creating a mysterious image. But why did Frances insist that this one photograph was genuine even after admitting that the others were faked? And what did she think she was photographing when she snapped that extra exposure?

So many questions, about a "solved" mystery! Small mysteries disappear once they've been solved, while great mysteries only grow deeper. It seems a safe bet that the Cottingley fairies will continue as a really great mystery. ∾

Disenchantment

LOUIS UNTERMEYER

Here in the German
Fairy forest;
And here I turn in,
I, the poorest
Son of an aging
Humble widow.
The light is fading;
Every shadow
Conceals a kobold,[1]
A gnome's dark eye,
Or even some troubled
Lorelei.[2]
A ruined castle
Invites me to prowl;
Its only vassal[3]
A frightened owl
(Most likely a princess
Under a spell)—
And what light dances
Behind that wall?
Perhaps great riches
Are hidden there,
Perhaps a witch's
Magic snare.
I walk up boldly,
Though my breath falters;
But no one holds me,

Nothing alters
Except the dying
Phosphorescence,[4]
Where the rocks lie in
Broken crescents.
These rocks are haunted,
Everyone says,
And here the enchanted
Dragon obeys
Only the youngest
Son of a widow,
Who waits the longest,
Fearing no shadow
Of any uncommon
Phantom in metal,

1 **kobold:** a gnome or spirit of German folklore
2 **Lorelei:** a woman of German legend whose
   singing lured boatmen to their deaths
3 **vassal:** servant

4 **phosphorescence:** radiance; brightness
5 **vespers:** a religious service held in the evenir

THE FAIRY WOOD
Henry Magnell Rheam

But dares to summon
The Thing to battle.
I've said my vespers,[5]
I've tightened my gloves;
The forest whispers
And chuckles and moves.
Darker and closer
The stillness surges.
Not even the ghost of
A rabbit emerges.
I rattle my weapons,
I call and I call
But nothing happens,
Nothing at all.

Nothing at all.

The Spring

PETER DICKINSON

When Derek was seven Great-Aunt Tessa had died and there'd been a funeral party for all the relations. In the middle of it a woman with a face like a sick fish, some kind of cousin, had grabbed hold of Derek and half-talked to him and half-talked to another cousin over his head.

"That's a handsome young fellow, aren't you? (Just like poor old Charlie, that age.) So you're young Derek. How old would you be now, then? (The girls—that's one of them, there, in the green blouse—they're a lot bigger.) Bit of an afterthought, weren't you, Derek? Nice surprise for your mum and dad. (Meg had been meaning to go back to that job of hers, you know . . .)"

And so on, just as if she'd been talking two languages, one he could understand and one he couldn't. Derek hadn't been surprised or shocked. In his heart he'd known all along.

It wasn't that anyone was unkind to him, or even uncaring. Of course his sisters sometimes called him a pest and told him to go away, but mostly the family included him in whatever they were doing and some-times, not just on his birthday, did something they thought would amuse him. But even those times Derek knew in his heart that he wasn't really meant to be there. If he'd never been born—well, like the cousin said, Mum would have gone back to her job full-time, and five years earlier too, and she'd probably have got promoted so there'd have been more money for things. And better holidays, sooner. And more room in the house—Cindy was always whining about having to share with Fran . . . It's funny to think about a world in which you've never existed, never been born. It would seem almost exactly the same to everyone else. They wouldn't miss you—there'd never have been anything for them to miss.

▲ ▲ ▲

About four years after Great-Aunt Tessa's funeral Dad got a new job and the family moved south. That June Dad and Mum took Derek off to look at a lot of roses. They had their new garden to fill, and there was this famous collection of roses only nine miles away at Something Abbey, so they could go and see if there were ones they specially liked, and get their order in for next winter. Mum and Dad were nuts about gardens. The girls had things of their own to do but it was a tagging-along afternoon for Derek.

The roses grew in a big walled garden, hundreds and hundreds of them, all different, with labels. Mum and Dad stood in front of each bush in turn, cocking their heads and pursing their lips while they decided if they liked it. They'd smell a bloom or two, and then Mum would read the label and Dad would look it up in his book to see if it was disease-resistant; last of all, Mum might write its name in her notebook and they'd give it marks, out of six, like skating judges, and move on. It took *hours*.

After a bit Mum remembered about Derek.

"Why don't you go down to the house and look at the river, darling? Don't fall in."

"Got your watch?" said Dad. "OK, back at the car park,[1] four-fifteen, sharp."

He gave Derek a pound[2] in case there were ice creams anywhere and turned back to the roses.

The river was better than the roses, a bit. The lawn of the big house ran down and became its bank. It was as wide as a road, not very deep but clear, with dark green weed streaming in the current and trout sometimes darting between. Derek found a twig and chucked it in, pacing beside it and timing its speed on his watch. He counted trout for a while, and then walking further along the river, he came to a strange shallow stream which ran through the lawns, like a winding path, only water, just a few inches deep but rushing through its channel in quick

1 **car park:** parking lot
2 **pound:** unit of money in England

ripples. Following it up, he came to a sort of hole in the ground, with a fence round it. The hole had stone sides and was full of water. The water came rushing up from somewhere underground, almost as though it were boiling. It was very clear. You could see a long way down.

While Derek stood staring, a group of other visitors strolled up and one of them started reading from her guidebook, gabbling[3] and missing bits out.

". . . remarkable spring . . . predates all the rest of the abbey . . . no doubt why the monks settled here . . . white chalk bowl fifteen feet across and twelve feet deep . . . crystal clear water surges out at about two hundred gallons a minute . . . always the same temperature, summer and winter . . ."

"Magical, don't you think?" said another of the tourists.

She didn't mean it. "Magical" was just a word to her. But yes, Derek thought, magical. Where does it come from? So close to the river, too, but it's got nothing to do with that. Perhaps it comes from another world.

He thought he'd only stood gazing for a short time, hypnotized by the rush of water welling and welling out of nowhere, but when he looked at his watch, it was ten past four. There was an ice-cream van, but Dad and Mum didn't get back to the car till almost twenty to five.

That night Derek dreamed about the spring. Nothing much happened in the dream, only he was standing beside it, looking down. It was night-time, with a full moon, and he was waiting for the moon to be reflected from the rumpled water. Something would happen then. He woke before it happened, with his heart hammering. He was filled with a sort of dread, though the dream hadn't been a nightmare. The dread was sort of neutral, halfway between terror and glorious excitement.

The same dream happened the next night, and the next, and the next. When it woke him on the fifth night, he thought this is getting to be a nuisance.

He got out of bed and went to the window. It was a brilliant night, with a full moon high. He felt wide awake. He turned from the window, meaning to get back into bed, but somehow found himself moving into his getting-up routine, taking his pajamas off and pulling on his shirt. The moment he realized what he was doing he stopped himself, but then thought why not? It'd fix that dream, at least. He laughed silently to himself and finished dressing. Ten minutes later he was bicycling through the dark.

3 **gabbling:** talking incoherently

Derek knew the way to the abbey because Mum was no use at map reading so that was something he did on car journeys—a way of joining in. He thought he could do it in an hour and a quarter, so he'd be there a bit after one. He'd be pretty tired by the time he got back, but the roads were flat down here compared with Yorkshire.[4] He'd left a note on the kitchen table saying "Gone for a ride. Back for breakfast." They'd think he'd just gone out for an early-morning spin—he was always first up. Nine miles there and nine back made eighteen. He'd done fifteen in one go last month. Shouldn't be too bad.

And in fact, although the night was still, he rode as though there were a stiff breeze at his back, hardly getting tired at all. Late cars swished through the dark. He tried to think of a story in case anyone stopped and asked what he was doing—if a police car came by, it certainly would— but no one did. He reached the abbey at ten past one. The gate was shut, of course. He hadn't even thought about getting in. There might be ivy, or something.

He found some a bit back along the way he'd come, but it wasn't strong or thick enough to climb. Still, it didn't cross his mind he wouldn't get in. He was going to. There would be a way.

The wall turned away from the road beside the garden of another house. Derek wheeled his bike through the gate and pushed it in among some bushes, then followed the wall back through the garden. No light shone from the house. Nobody stirred. He followed the wall of the abbey grounds along toward the back of the garden. He thought he could hear the river rustling beyond. The moonlight was very bright, casting shadows so black they looked solid. The garden became an orchard, heavy old trees, their leafy branches blotting out the moon, but with a clear space further on. Ducking beneath the branches, he headed toward it. The night air smelt of something new, sweetish, familiar— fresh-cut sawdust. When he reached the clear space, he found it surrounded a tree trunk which had had all its branches cut off and just stood there like a twisted arm sticking out of the ground. Leaning against it was a ladder.

It wasn't very heavy. Derek carried it over to the abbey wall. It reached almost to the top. He climbed, straddled the wall, leaned down, and with an effort hauled the ladder up and lowered it on the further side, down into the darkness under the trees that grew there, then

---

4 **Yorkshire:** county in northern England

climbed down and groped his way out toward where the moonlight gleamed between the tree trunks. Out in the open on the upper slope of lawn he got his bearings, checked for a landmark so that he would be able to find his way back to the ladder, and walked down in the shadow of the trees toward the river. His heart was beginning to thump, the way it did in the dream. The same dread, between terror and glory, seemed to bubble up inside him.

When he was level with the spring he walked across the open and stood by the low fence, gazing down at the troubled water. It looked very black, and in this light he couldn't see into it at all. He tried to find the exact place he had stood in the dream, and waited. A narrow rim of moon-shadow cast by the wall on the left side edged the disk of water below. It thinned and thinned as the slow-moving moon heeled west. And now it was gone.

The reflection of the moon, broken and scattered by the endlessly upswelling water, began to pass glimmeringly across the disk below. Derek could feel the turn of the world making it move like that. His heartbeat came in hard pulses, seeming to shake his body. Without knowing what he was doing, he climbed the fence and clung to its inner side so that he could gaze straight down into the water. His own reflection, broken by the ripples, was a squat black shape against the silver moonlight. He crouched with his left arm clutching the lowest rail and with his right arm strained down toward it. He could just reach. The black shape changed as the reflection of his arm came to meet it. The water was only water to his touch.

Somehow he found another three inches of stretch and plunged his hand through the surface. The water was still water, but then another hand gripped his.

He almost lost his balance and fell, but the other hand didn't try to pull him in. It didn't let go either. When Derek tried to pull free the hand came with him, and an arm behind it. He pulled, heaved, strained. A head broke the surface. Another arm reached up and gripped the top of the side wall. Now Derek could straighten and take a fresh hold higher up the fence. And now the stranger could climb out, gasping and panting, over the fence and stand on the moonlit lawn beside him. He was a boy about Derek's own age, wearing ordinary clothes like Derek's. They were dry to the touch.

"I thought you weren't coming," said the boy. "Have we got somewhere to live?"

"I suppose you'd better come home."

They walked together toward the trees.

"Who . . . ?" began Derek.

"Not now," said the stranger.

They stole on in silence. We'll have to walk the whole way home, thought Derek. Mightn't get in before breakfast. How'm I going to explain?

The ladder was still against the wall. They climbed it, straddled the top, lowered the ladder on the far side, and climbed down, propping it back against its tree. Then back toward the road.

There were two bikes hidden in the bushes.

"How on . . . ?" began Derek.

"Not now," said the stranger.

They biked in silence the whole way home, getting in just as the sky was turning gray. They took off their shoes and tiptoed up the stairs. Derek was so tired he couldn't remember going to bed.

▲ ▲ ▲

They were woken by Cindy's call outside the door.

"Hi! Pests! Get up! School bus in twenty mins!"

Derek scrambled into his clothes and just beat David down the stairs. Dad was in the hallway, looking through the post[5] before driving off to work.

"Morning, twins," he said. "Decided to have a lie-in?"[6]

They gobbled their breakfast and caught the bus by running. Jimmy Grove had kept two seats for them. He always did.

▲ ▲ ▲

Very occasionally during that year Derek felt strange. There was something not quite right in the world, something out of balance, some shadow. It was like that feeling you have when you think you've glimpsed something out of the corner of your eye but when you turn your head it isn't there. Once or twice it was so strong he almost said something. One evening, for instance, he and David were sitting either side of Mum while she leafed through an old photograph album. They laughed or groaned at pictures of themselves as babies, or in fancy dress—Tweedledum and Tweedledee[7]—and then Mum pointed at a picture of an old woman with

5 **post:** mail

6 **have a lie in:** sleep in

7 **Tweedledum and Tweedledee:** twins from *Alice in Wonderland*

a crooked grinning face, like a jolly witch, and said, "I don't suppose you remember her. That's Great-Aunt Tessa. You went to her funeral."

"I remember the funeral," said David. "There was a grisly sort of cousin who grabbed us and told us how handsome we were, and then talked over our heads about us to someone else as if we couldn't understand what she was saying."

"She had a face like a sick fish," said Derek.

"Oh, Cousin Vi. She's a pain in the neck. She . . ."

And Mum rattled on about Cousin Vi's murky doings for a bit and then turned the page, but for a moment Derek felt that he had almost grasped the missing whatever-it-was, almost turned his head quick enough to see something before it vanished. No.

On the whole it was a pretty good year. There were dud bits.[8] David broke a leg in the Easter hols,[9] which spoilt things for a while. The girls kept complaining that the house wasn't big enough for seven, especially with the pests growing so fast, but then Jackie got a job and went to live with friends in a flat in Totton. Dad bought a new car. Those were the most exciting things that happened, so it was a nothing-much year, but not bad. And then one weekend in June Mum and Dad went off to the abbey to look at the roses again. Cindy and Fran were seeing friends, so it was just the twins who tagged along.

The roses were the same as last year, and Mum and Dad slower than ever, so after a bit David said, "Let's go and look at the river. OK, Mum?"

Dad gave them money for ices[10] and told them when to be back at the car. They raced twigs on the river, tried to spot the largest trout, and then found the stream that ran through the lawn and followed it up to the spring. They stood staring at the uprushing water for a long while, not saying anything. In the end Derek looked at his watch, saw it was almost four, woke David from his trance and raced him off to look for ices.

▲ ▲ ▲

A few nights later Derek woke with his heart pounding. It was something he'd dreamt, but he couldn't remember the dream. He sat up and saw that David's bed was empty. When he got up and put his hand between the sheets, they were still just warm to the touch.

8 **dud bits:** bad or boring periods

9 **hols:** holidays

10 **ices:** frozen desserts composed of ice and fruit juice

All at once memory came back, the eleven years when he'd been on his own and the year when he'd had David. The other years, the ones when he'd been growing up with a twin brother and the photographs in the album had been taken—they weren't real. By morning he wouldn't remember them. By morning he wouldn't remember David either. There was just this one night.

He rushed into his clothes, crept down the stairs and out. The door was unlocked. David's bike was already gone from the shed. He got his own out and started off.

The night was still, but he felt as though he had an intangible wind in his face. Every pedal stroke was an effort. He put his head down and rode on. Normally, he knew, he'd be faster than David, whose leg still wasn't properly strong after his accident, but tonight he guessed David would have the spirit wind behind him, the wind from some other world. Derek didn't think he would catch him. All he knew was that he had to try.

In fact he almost ran into him, about two miles from the abbey, just after the turn off the main road. David was trotting along beside his bike, pushing it, gasping for breath.

"What's happened?" said Derek.

"Got a puncture. Lend me yours. I'll be too late."

"Get up behind. We'll need us both to climb the wall. There mayn't be a ladder this time."

Without a word David climbed onto the saddle. Derek stood on the pedals and drove the bike on through the dark. They leaned the bike against the wall where the ivy grew. It still wasn't thick enough to climb, but it was something to get a bit of a grip on. David stood on the saddle of the bike. Derek put his hands under his heels and heaved him up, grunting with the effort, till David could grip the coping[11] of the wall. He still couldn't pull himself right up, but he found a bit of a foothold in the ivy and hung there while Derek climbed onto the crossbar, steadied himself, and let David use his shoulder as a step. A heave, a scrabble, and he was on the wall.

Derek stood on the saddle and reached up. He couldn't look, but felt David reach down to touch his hand, perhaps just to say good-bye. Derek gripped the hand and held. David heaved. Scrabbling and stretching, Derek leaped for the coping. He heard the bike clatter away beneath

11 **coping:** the top covering of a wall

him. David's other hand grabbed his collar. He had an elbow on the coping, and now a knee, and he was up.

"Thanks," he muttered.

The drop on the far side was into blackness. There could have been anything below, but there seemed no help for it. You just had to hang from the coping, let go and trust to luck. Derek landed on softness but wasn't ready for the impact and stumbled, banging his head against the wall. He sat down, his whole skull filled with the pain of it. Dimly he heard a sort of crash, and as the pain seeped away worked out that David must have fallen into a bush. More cracks and rustles as David struggled free.

"Are you OK?" came his voice.

"Think so. Hit my head."

"Where are you?"

"I'm OK. Let's get on."

They struggled out through a sort of shrubbery, making enough noise, it seemed, to wake all Hampshire.[12] Derek's head was just sore on the outside now. Blood was running down his cheek. David was already running, a dark limping shape about twenty yards away. His leg must have gone duff[13] again after all that effort. Derek followed him across the moonlit slopes and levels. They made no effort to hide. If anyone had been watching from the house they must have seen them, the moonlight was so strong. At last they stood panting by the fence of the spring. The rim of shadow still made a thin line under a wall.

"Done it," whispered David. "I thought I was stuck."

"What'd have happened?"

"Don't know."

"What's it like . . . the other side?"

"Different. Shhh."

The shadow vanished and the reflection of the moon moved onto the troubled disk. Derek glanced sideways at his brother's face. The rippled, reflected light glimmered across it, making it very strange, gray white like a mushroom, and changing all the time as the ripples changed, as if it wasn't even sure of its own proper shape.

David climbed the fence, grasped the bottom rail, and lowered his legs into the water. Derek climbed too, gripped David's hand, and crouched to lower his brother—yes, his brother still—his last yard in this world.

---

12 **Hampshire:** county in southern England
13 **duff:** slang for bad or worthless

David let go of the rail and dropped. Derek gripped his hand all the way to the water.

As he felt that silvery touch the movement stopped, and they hung there, either side of the rippled mirror. David didn't seem to want to let go, either.

Different? thought Derek. Different how?

The hand wriggled, impatient. Something must be happening the other side. No time to make up his mind. He let go of the rail.

In the instant that he plunged toward the water he felt a sort of movement around him, very slight, but clear. It was the whole world closing in, filling the gap where he had been. In that instant, he realized everything changed. Jackie would still be at home, Fran would be asleep in his room, not needing to share with Cindy. Nobody would shout at him to come to breakfast. His parents would go about their day with no sense of loss; Jimmy Grove would keep no place for him on the school bus; Mum would be a director of her company, with a car of her own . . . and all the photographs in the albums would show the same cheerful family, two parents, three daughters, no gap, not even the faintest shadow that might once have been Derek.

He was leaving a world where he had never been born. ∾

RIPPLED SURFACE
1950
M.C. Escher

Caleb's Colors

Neal Shusterman

A dark hat. A dark coat. A tall figure standing in the doorway, silhouetted by the stark streetlight.

"My name is Quentin Prax. I'm here about your son."

I didn't like him. Not at first. The way he spoke, it was so slow, so practiced and smooth. The way he said his name—hissing it like a snake. *Praxsssssss.*

"We've been expecting you," said my father.

The man stepped into the light of the living room, where I could see that his dark coat was not black but brown. Not just brown though—it was woven of many different colors, all intertwined until they blended perfectly into a rich mahogany. His eyes locked on mine, and he smiled. I had to look away. His smile was unnerving.[1] It could not be read. Like his coat, it seemed to be woven of so many different thoughts and meanings that I didn't know what that smile was for.

"You must be the sister," he said to me through that smile.

I didn't like being called "the sister." "My name's Rhia," I told him. He smiled again.

"Rhia. What a colorful name."

He strolled across our living room as if he were welcome, and my parents didn't do anything about it. His presence was so powerful, my parents had no response.

Prax turned to Caleb, my little brother. Caleb sat at the kitchen table, the place he could most often be found, with a box of Crayolas. His left hand moved across a piece of paper, leaving periwinkle streaks.

---

1 **unnerving:** aggravating; upsetting

When you first watch Caleb and his Crayolas, you might think his marks are random—just wild firings from a ruined brain—but watch long enough, and you'll see shapes forming out of those wild lines, until you suddenly realize that you're looking at a sailing ship, or a mountain range, or a lion that seems so real you'd swear it might leap off the page at you.

And Caleb does all this without even looking at the page. He'll just sit there, staring forward, rocking back and forth, in a way that could make you seasick just watching him.

"This must be Caleb," said Mr. Prax. "How are you, Caleb?"

"He won't answer you," I told the man. "He doesn't talk."

But Mr. Prax only smiled that many-colored smile once more and said, "Oh, he does. He just doesn't care to use words." I tried to stare this Mr. Prax down, but I couldn't. People who came to help Caleb promised us the moon, then they took our money and left Caleb no better than they found him. Caleb's condition gave my parents enough to fight about without having to argue over quack doctors—which is exactly what I figured Prax was. He smiled at me again, then he turned to my parents. "May we talk in private?"

"Rhia," said my mother, "why don't you take Caleb upstairs and get him ready for bed."

I was irritated that I couldn't be a part of whatever was going on, but also relieved that I could be out of Mr. Prax's sight. I didn't trust him. He seemed far too calculating and mysterious. I didn't like mysteries—especially when they were strutting around my house.

I took Caleb's hand and lifted him to his feet. He followed me upstairs quietly tonight. Sometimes it's not so easy. Sometimes he would whine and pull his hair. Sometimes he would scream like the end of the world had come. I had grown used to all of that—I had had to, because putting him to bed was a responsibility I had chosen to take on. But tonight he didn't kick and scream; he merely followed.

I took him to his room and dressed him for bed. All the time he stared forward with that blank, nonseeing look of his. He could stare for hours at the TV like that, and I always wondered what he saw there. Light and colors? Shapes moving back and forth? There were times when he would take a crayon to paper and recreate, line for line, the image of something he had seen on TV, as if his mind was a VCR, recording everything it saw. Then there would be the times he would draw things too strange and exotic to have come from anywhere in this world. In one moment he

would draw a place of terror so dark I could not bear to look at it, and then in the next instant turn the page over and draw a world of such intense beauty it would make me truly know that there was a God somewhere, because who else could put such a beautiful image into the head of a small, autistic[2] boy?

That was life with Caleb. A never-ending gallery of Crayola wonders that papered the wall of his room, floor to ceiling. Me, I could barely draw a stick figure . . . but it didn't make me jealous. How could I be jealous of a brother whose whole world had no room for anything but himself and his Crayolas?

I finished dressing Caleb for bed and left him. Sneaking out onto the stairs, I peeked down into the kitchen, where Mr. Prax sat with my parents.

"I've done much work with idiot savants," said Mr. Prax. I bristled at the expression "idiot savant." That's the label the world gives people like Caleb. People whose brain somehow got wired to do one thing and one thing only. There were people who could do instant math like a supercomputer but had to be taught to feed themselves. There were some who could memorize hundreds of books just by skimming through them but couldn't hold a conversation. I'd even heard of a little girl labeled as severely retarded who designed an aircraft for the military.

Dad sat with his arms crossed. Mom had called Prax on the advice of a friend, but it had been a long time since Dad trusted therapists.

"Caleb's had every therapy in the book," said Dad. "I doubt yours will help any more than the others did."

"You don't understand," said Mr. Quentin Prax sharply. "I'm not here as a therapist, I'm here as an employer. I'm the owner of a small but prestigious art gallery specializing in unique works of art. Perhaps you've heard of it: the Galleria du Mondes."[3]

My parents seemed as surprised as I was. If he wasn't a doctor, then what did he want with Caleb?

"We don't know of it," admitted my mother. "We're not really art patrons . . ."

"My gallery seeks out . . . special artists with unique talents," Prax told them. "A colleague[4] of mine came across one of Caleb's sketches and sent it to me. I was quite impressed."

---

2 **autistic:** one with autism, a mental disorder characterized by repetitive behavior, language problems, and the inability to interact with others

3 **Galleria du Mondes:** Gallery of the Worlds

4 **colleague:** coworker; a person who works in the same profession

Mom stiffened in her chair. Until now she had watched Prax with wide and hopeful eyes. But now it seemed her hope was draining fast.

"Just what is it you want, Mr. Prax?" she said coldly.

Prax grinned at her. "Simple," he said. "I would like to commission a large work from him."

Mom laughed, and Dad, well, he just got angry.

"Listen," said my father. "We've got a little boy with a lot of problems. I don't like the idea of hiring him out as some sort of creative freak for the amusement of a bunch of snobs."

Mr. Prax looked down at his perfectly manicured fingernails, unconcerned with my father's anger. "You misunderstand," he said. "The sole purpose of my gallery is to give expression to creativity that would otherwise be lost. Your son has a gift, and I'd like to help him share it with the world." Mr. Prax paused for a moment, then took a deep breath and said, "I have a special interest, you see, because my own daughter was very much like your boy."

"Was?" questioned Mom.

"She's no longer with me."

"I'm sorry," said Mom.

My father sighed, on the verge of giving in. "How much will this cost?" he asked.

Mr. Prax laughed heartily at that—loud enough that it made me jump. "It won't cost you, my friend, it will only cost me," he said. Then he pulled an envelope out of his pocket and handed it to my father, who opened it and began laughing. There was a check in the envelope.

"All right, who put you up to this?" he chuckled. "Was it Joe at work? He's always pulling practical jokes."

"No joke," said Prax, completely serious. "And that's only half. The other half is payable on completion of the work."

My mother was gasping as if she were hyperventilating.[5]

"A million dollars? For a drawing by Caleb?"

"My gallery has some very wealthy patrons."

I could hardly believe it myself. I thought of the way Mom and Dad always bought those stupid lottery tickets, even though a person's more likely to get struck by lightning five times than to win once—and now the jackpot comes walking right into our living room.

---

5 **hyperventilating:** breathing rapidly

"I'm sure Caleb's condition has left you with a great many medical expenses," reminded Prax. "This will pay those expenses with more than enough left over for you."

Well, Caleb might not talk, but money does, and Mr. Prax had himself a deal. As they came walking out of the kitchen, I tried to scoot up the stairs, into the shadows, where I couldn't be seen—but Prax saw me nonetheless. He stared at me with that strange smile again.

"Rhia," said Mr. Prax. "I would very much like you to come to my gallery and assist your brother in his creation."

I shrunk back even further.

"I don't do what he does," I told him.

"Of course not," said Prax. "But every artist needs an assistant."

"No," I told him. I wouldn't be bought, like my parents were.

My parents turned to me in shock, as if I had just thrown a stone through a plate glass window, then my mother turned back to Mr. Prax.

"Rhia will be happy to go," declared my mother. Then she turned to me. "After all, it's summer vacation, so she has plenty of time, don't you, Rhia?"

I didn't trust this Mr. Prax, no matter how much money he had. He wasn't just a rich guy who liked to help autistic kids—there was much more to him than that. Still, this was a battle I knew I couldn't win. Three adults and a million dollars against little ol' me. No matter how far I wanted to be away from Prax, I knew I was destined to spend days, maybe weeks, with the eerie man, watching Caleb paint.

"Fine," I said. "I'll go, but only because I want to make sure Caleb's treated right."

"Splendid," said Prax. "I'd like Caleb and Rhia at my gallery at nine o'clock sharp tomorrow morning."

After Mr. Prax had gone, I went back up to Caleb's room, where he sat on the edge of his bed, exactly where I'd left him.

I stretched him out and pulled the covers over him. He lay there looking up at the ceiling—a ceiling that was covered with his Crayola creations.

"Do you know you're worth a million dollars, Caleb," I said to him. He blinked, but showed no signs of hearing me. "Do you even know what a million dollars is?" Still no response. I don't know why I always expected him to say something.

"Good night, Caleb. I love you." I turned off the light, went to my room, and slipped into a sleep filled with nightmares I couldn't remember.

▲ ▲ ▲

Caleb and I took a bus to Mr. Prax's gallery, but instead of bringing us inside, he took us for a ride in his white Mercedes limousine. The limousine, he told us, was a gift from one of the clients of his gallery. I wondered how anyone—even a rich person—could give away a limousine.

We drove for an hour, into the heart of the city, until we stopped at an immense museum of art. All afternoon we wandered through the maze of exhibits.

"See how Manet uses light to capture the moment of sunset here," Prax said at one point. "See how Van Gogh's thick textures bring the night sky to life," he said at another. "See how the tiny points of color in Seurat's work blend together the farther away you stand."[6] Gallery after gallery, he had something to say about every artist, every painting, until my mind was so full of color and texture that all I could see was gray.

"Why are you doing this?" I finally asked him. "Caleb doesn't care. He's not listening to you. He doesn't know a Monet from a Manet from a Schmanet. He's retarded." I hated the word, but I was angry. "He's worse than retarded. Don't you understand that?"

Then he looked at me with that same cold stare he gave my father the night before. "I'm not talking to him. I'm talking to *you*."

"Me?"

I looked at Caleb, whose eyes wandered around, giving as much time to the thermostat on the wall as they did to the paintings.

"Caleb needs no words to tell him about these paintings," said Mr. Prax.

"So why are you telling me about it?" I asked.

"So that maybe you'll be able to understand some of the things he already knows," was Prax's answer. Then he asked me something I'll never forget.

"Do you think that these artists were masters?"

"Sure," I said. "I guess."

Prax shook his head. "No. These artists could only bring a hint of greatness to their canvases. Shadows of possibilities, nothing more. They are failures." And then he leaned in close to me. "Would you like to see the work of real masters?"

---

6 **Manet … Van Gogh … Seurat:** European painters of the Impressionist period

And although I didn't want to go anywhere else with Mr. Prax today, curiosity had already begun to drill deep into my brain. I nodded my head and said, "Yes. Yes I do."

▲ ▲ ▲

He took us back to his gallery, where the walls were covered with canvases filled with dripping splotches of brown paint.

"You call these masterpieces?" I asked. "Looks like a lot of mud to me."

He shook his head. "This isn't the gallery. The real gallery is upstairs."

He opened a door and took us up a narrow staircase into a huge loft. It must have once been a factory or something, because it had brick walls, and lots of windows—but those windows were all painted over.

Surrounding us were dozens upon dozens of sheet-covered canvases, all five- or six-feet tall, and all resting upon heavy wooden easels. In the dim light of the huge loft, they looked like ghosts all facing in different directions.

He locked the door behind us.

"These are the works of the masters," he said and began to pull away the sheets that covered them one by one.

Any doubts I had were gone the moment I laid eyes on that first canvas.

It was a landscape like nothing I had ever seen, and trying to explain it now is like trying to explain sight to a blind person. These were colors the human eye had never before seen. Colors that had no names, depicting a place too strange and surreal to be of this world.

The second masterpiece was in a different set of hues, but just as incredible: A scene of clouds billowing upward toward a sun that actually shone, lighting up the room. Deep within the painting, golden winged beings seemed caught in a glorious journey toward that sun.

The third was the most magnificent of all. A forest of impossibly exotic trees, swirling in a greenish mist. Hills rolled into the distance, and in the foreground the single limb of a tree curved downward, with a smattering of red leaves. It seemed so real I could almost smell the rich fragrances of the forest and feel the slow breeze that made the mist swim and shimmer. It was unearthly, and otherworldly, like the other paintings.

"You wish to touch the painting," said Prax. It wasn't so much a question as a statement of fact. "You may do so. These paintings are meant to be touched."

I reached out toward one of those redder-than-red leaves to feel its velvet texture . . .

. . . and when I drew my hand away, I was holding the leaf between my fingers!

I gasped, and let the leaf flutter to the ground.

Prax smiled. "The task of the artists," he said, "is the creation of worlds. Very few succeed. Many die trying."

▲　▲　▲

In a small room behind the great gallery was a paint-splattered studio, and in that studio were a palette, brushes, and about a thousand brand-new tubes of paint. All set up in front of a canvas the same size as the others in the gallery. Only this canvas was empty.

Caleb stood just a few inches away from the canvas, staring that blank stare of his, and Mr. Prax put a paintbrush in Caleb's hand.

"Do you believe in miracles, Rhia?"

To be honest, I didn't know. But then my brother began to paint. Thick, heavy brush strokes. In moments Caleb had begun creating a bright, wonderful work of art.

Then I saw something out of the corner of my eye. There was something shiny in Prax's hand. Shiny and sharp. I gasped and pulled Caleb away from the canvas as Prax brought the carving knife down . . . slashing through the center of the canvas. The fabric shredded from top to bottom.

"No!" he screamed furiously at Caleb. "Look at those brush strokes! This is Van Gogh!" I was so shocked, all I could do was push myself back against the wall in disbelief.

Caleb screamed as if he himself had been stabbed and didn't stop screaming until Prax brought another canvas. He quieted immediately and silently resumed painting. He dabbed his brush against the canvas lightly, creating tiny little points of light. Again Prax's knife came down, shredding the emerging work.

"No!" Prax yelled. "This is Seurat."

Caleb wailed again and began to rock feverishly back and forth. Once more Prax brought a fresh canvas.

I wanted to grab Caleb and run, taking him away from this ranting, insane man—and yet part of me must have understood what he was doing, and why he was doing it. Because I stayed. I stayed to witness Caleb's terrifying ordeal.

"We're not leaving here," shouted Prax, "until we're done. Even if it takes days. Weeks. Months."

On and on it went. I began crying, begging Prax to stop, but he wouldn't. He shredded canvas after canvas—one that looked like a Manet, and another like a Picasso. Caleb barely had a chance to get down a single brush stroke before that awful knife would come down again, sending him into a screaming fit, each one worse than the one before.

And then Caleb just shut down.

Prax put a new canvas in front of him, and Caleb didn't move. He stood there, red in the face, staring at the white fabric with an expression of emptiness worse than ever before—as if he were staring through the canvas with no emotion. No mind. He didn't even try to paint.

"Now you've done it!" I shouted at Prax through my tears. "Now he'll never paint or pick up a crayon ever again! You've ruined the one thing he can do, you monster."

Prax didn't answer me; he just looked at Caleb, waiting. Then I heard the faraway jingling of bells, and Prax left to greet a customer who had just arrived downstairs. He closed the door behind him, and Caleb and I were alone with the horribly empty canvas.

"Caleb," I whispered. "Caleb, you don't have to paint. You don't have to do anything. We'll get you home. I'll tuck you in bed. It'll be just like it always was. You'd like that, wouldn't you?"

Nothing. Caleb didn't even rock back and forth. Something was very, very wrong, and I cursed Prax for doing this to him.

That's when I heard voices outside the door. I peeked through the keyhole to see Prax—his slick, smooth self leading a couple through the great secret gallery. The man and woman hardly looked rich enough to invest in great works of art. In fact, they looked poor, worn, and tired, as if they'd seen more trouble and pain than most.

The man knelt down on the gallery floor, opened up a suitcase, and showed its contents to Prax.

"It's all there," said the man wearily. "Every penny we could find. Everything we own."

"I'm afraid it's not very much," the woman apologized.

Prax waved the remark away. I guess he didn't care how much it was. "Have you chosen a work that suits you?" he asked.

The man and woman stepped toward the surreal landscape with the red leaves.

"Ah," said Prax, smiling his multicolored smile for them. "My daughter's. I hope you enjoy it."

And with that I could see the look of world-weariness leave the couple's faces. How would they carry it out, I wondered—it was such a huge canvas.

I leaned back to brush some hair from my face, and when I peeked through the hole again, the couple was gone . . .

. . . and a single leaf, redder than red, fluttered to the floor at Prax's feet. My heart missed a very long beat.

Prax immediately covered the painting with a sheet, and turned.

"Come out, Rhia," he said, knowing I was there all along. "The door isn't locked."

I stepped into the gallery and helped Mr. Prax adjust the sheet on the painting so it hung just right.

Prax seemed to sigh in satisfaction, then closed the suitcase. I noticed it only seemed to have a few crumpled bills.

"This world we live in," said Prax, "is kind to some, but cruel to others. For those who would rather not be here, I provide . . . alternatives." Then he smiled at me, and although his smile still seemed filled with many strange colors, I felt I could understand some of them now. "Perhaps there will come a time," he said, "when everyone will have to choose a masterpiece."

The smell of oil paint seemed to grow stronger around me, and I turned to see that Caleb had begun painting. He was working feverishly—and this time it was different from before. As I stepped back into the studio, I could see the speed at which his fingers were moving. They were a blur. Even the colors he was putting on that canvas seemed far brighter, far more special than the colors that came from the tubes of paint.

All the time he stared through that white canvas as if the work was already there behind it and he wasn't so much brushing on paint as he was brushing away the emptiness. Soon he threw the paintbrush away and began to use his fingers, spreading and blending the colors from corner to corner. For half an hour we watched in awed silence, and half an hour was all it took.

"My God!" I said when it was done, but my words seemed far away, lost in the depth of the painting.

It was something entirely new, nothing like what any artist anywhere had ever created. The world Caleb had made was both wilderness and city, both earth and sky. Wild winds swept through magnificent trees toward gleaming crystalline spires.[7] Brilliant shafts of light spilled upon peaceful hills, and yet the light was balanced by deep shafts of darkness that swam with unknowable mysteries. Still, as new as all this was, it was somehow familiar. It was then that I realized that everything in this great work I'd seen before. A fragment on the refrigerator door. A sketch on Caleb's wall. Everything Caleb had ever drawn was just a shadow of this, his great work. His one work.

I reached toward it, wanting more than anything to reach into it—and instead I got my fingers covered with paint.

Caleb smoothed over the smudge I had made with my fingers.

"It's not finished," said Mr. Prax. "It needs a signature."

"But Caleb can't write his name."

Mr. Prax shook his head. "That's not the kind of signature I mean." Then Prax leaned over and whispered into Caleb's ear. "Go on, Caleb. Finish it."

And with that, Caleb reached forward and pressed his spread fingers against the center of his creation. He grit his teeth. He squinted his eyes and pushed that hand against the canvas with all his soul, until finally his hand punched through . . . into a world rich with colors. I could see the canvas changing, the flatness of it stretching out and back like a wave was rolling through it, until its depth reached the infinite horizon.

Caleb looked at his fingers there inside of his painting, watching the light playing off of them . . . then he lurched forward and leapt into it. Once inside, he threw his hands out. He spun around. He was dancing— Caleb was actually dancing! And then for the first time in his life he turned his head to look at me. And he smiled. It was a smile filled with more colors than Mr. Prax's. That's when I knew Caleb was finally where he belonged. Caleb didn't waste time saying good-bye. He turned and ran, hopped and skipped deep into his world, until he disappeared in a place the canvas did not show.

My joy to have seen him so happy overwhelmed my grief at knowing he was gone. With my eyes full of tears, I reached my hand into that world too. I felt the warmth of that strange light. How I wanted to launch myself in there as well, but Mr. Prax had something else in mind.

"I need a gatekeeper," he told me. "Someone to decide whom Caleb would want in his world. Will you do that for me?"

7 **crystalline spires:** glass steeples

I didn't answer him. Instead I went to a shelf, opened a sheet, and together we gently covered the canvas.

▲ ▲ ▲

That night we brought Mom and Dad to the gallery, to show them the masterpiece—and although my parents can be thick as a brick sometimes, one look at the painting and they understood. My mother cried tears of both joy and loss, as I had. My father hid his feelings by comforting her.

Since then, I've been taking my own art lessons. I still don't know much about art, but I do know that there are places inside of us—palaces of glorious light and caverns of unknowable darkness. Magical places filled with brilliant, unimaginable colors that we suffer to bring forth.

I know I could never suffer the way Caleb did—to imagine a place so perfectly that it becomes real—but if someday I can paint just a shadow of the possibilities . . . perhaps that will be enough. ∾

RESPONDING TO CLUSTER THREE

WHAT'S REAL AND HOW DO YOU KNOW?

Thinking Skill EVALUATING

1. Study the photograph of the "fairy" on page 80. Are you surprised that so many people were fooled? Why or why not?

2. Write a short **character sketch** of Mr. Prax that would describe him to someone who has not read "Caleb's Colors." Describe both his outward appearance as well as other characteristics such as his voice and his apparent attitude toward others.

3. Rhia, the narrator of "Caleb's Colors," **evaluates** Mr. Prax from the very beginning of the story. Find at least three quotations that show her feelings about Mr. Prax at the beginning, middle, and end of the story.

4. Add the selections in this cluster to the classification chart you started at the end of Cluster One.

5. All of the selections in this cluster have elements of both **reality** and **fantasy.** Use a chart such as the one below to list some of these elements. Then add at least one item or event that seems to combine reality and fantasy.

Selection	Real things	Fantasy	Combination
"Ticing" the Fairies			
The Spring			
Caleb's Colors			
Disenchantment			

Writing Activity: Memo to the Editor-in-Chief

Suppose that all of the selections in this cluster were sent to you by hopeful authors. Your job as editorial assistant for a fantasy magazine is to **evaluate** the selections, choose your favorite, and write a memo to the editor-in-chief recommending it for publishing. To help with your selection, first establish your criteria for a good fantasy story. You may want to refer to the definition of fantasy you wrote for Cluster One.

Your Evaluation Memo Should

- begin with the purpose of your memo
- list the criteria you used in making your selection
- list the key reasons for your positive evaluation
- offer to provide further information and/or request a reply
- use language that is courteous, precise, and business-like

CLUSTER FOUR

Thinking on Your Own
Thinking Skill SYNTHESIZING

Black Angel

Nancy Springer

*T*imes were tough for the Jersey Devil. Hoofprints on the housetops, which were enough to win his South Devon granddaddy[1] uproar and a place in the history books back in 1855, went all but unnoticed in the Garden State in the days since the New Jersey Turnpike had replaced the supernatural as most Jerseyites' personal experience of hell. When something screamed like a woman in the pine barrens, Jersey dwellers assumed it was a woman, presumably a New Yorker, screaming in the pine barrens. Few humans, even young humans, bothered to stray into the ever-shrinking sand-and-scrub wilds of south Jersey anymore; for adventure, they preferred Nintendo. What was a weird manifestation[2] to do for attention? Not to speak of food. Few people kept chickens in their backyards anymore. What was a meat-eating equine[3] to do for blood? Hooves were not meant for hunting.

What a bite. Skulking in the moonlit scrub along a secondary highway, searching for a nice fresh roadkill but affronted by the odor of rancid opossum, the Jersey Devil indulged in despondent and rebellious thoughts. *Why do I even bother with the rules anymore? There's no respect for monsters left in the world. Life has lost all meaning, all mystery. How can I compete with TV? I might as well start showing myself in daylight and be done with it.*

---

1 **South Devon granddaddy:** a reference to a historical account of horselike footprints left in Devon, a county in southwestern England, in 1855.

2 **manifestation:** a ghost or dweller of the underworld

3 **equine:** horse

"A horse!" whispered a breathy, youthful female voice.

In the shadow of a scrub pine the Jersey Devil froze, outraged to be caught by surprise but even more outraged to be mistaken for a common horse. *Can't you see the red fire of my eyes in the darkness? Can't you see how blackly I loom?*

What are you doing out here?

The pine barrens, or what pitiful remnants were left of the pine barrens, belonged to creature denizens at night. By the rules, the human had to be frightened away. Lifting a head worthy of an equine gargoyle, stretching his heavy, muscular neck, and working his bulky chest like a bellows, the Jersey Devil let out his distinctive scream, a warning as chilling as a panther's screech.

"What's the matter, horsie?" The girl pattered forward from the shadows. "I love horses," she said in soft, exalted tones. "What's the matter? Are you caught in that bush?" The nincompoop seemed to have taken his challenge as a squall for help. Exactly what sort of brain damage was this human suffering? "Oh!" She stopped where she stood, a preadolescent wraith[4] in the moonlight. "Oh," she breathed in tones yet more hushed, more rapt, "oh, wings! You're a Pegasus! Oh!"

Poised to scream again, the Jersey Devil gave an undignified grunt of surprise instead. Surprise and sneaking gratification. He had always felt, though never daring to do more than think it, that he was at least as worthy of immortalization as Pegasus.[5] Why should a beautiful white, grass-eating horse with wings be considered a major-league mythological creature, while a not-so-beautiful black, meat-eating horse with wings—bat wings—was considered a monster, and a minor one at that? It was unfair. It was discrimination.

This girl was obviously exceptionally intelligent among humans. The Jersey Devil lowered his rawboned head to regard her with unwonted[6] interest. There she stood, fearless, a skinny child in owlish glasses, her clothing skimpy and cottony and undistinguished, her feet bare and curled in protest against the pine needles—he noticed the pallor of her feet in the moonlight, small fishlike surfaces even whiter than the south Jersey sand. Why did humans have such soft and inadequate feet? Dependent upon shoes. How pitiful.

---

4 **wraith:** ghostlike figure

5 **Pegasus:** a winged horse of Greek mythology

6 **unwonted:** unaccustomed; unusual

"I must be hungrier than I thought," the girl murmured. "I seem to be seeing things." She stepped forward until she stood directly by the Jersey Devil's shoulder, her soft feet inches from his hooves, her scrawny hand reaching for him. He shuddered at her touch yet was so fascinated by her lack of fear that he did not move either to escape or resist that fumbling contact. "No, they're real," she whispered, stroking the leather of his wings.

Her touch was as weak as her voice. Her lack of fear was perhaps due to—what? Had something driven her out here, to the darkness, the wilderness? Out of her home and out of her mind? Some extremity?[7]

"I guess somebody heard me after all," she said. "They sent me a horse angel."

Oh, sure. Give me a break.

"What are you doing stuck in this bush?" she asked the Jersey Devil. "Are you okay?" She limped around his head to scout the other side of him, running her hand down his neck. Crouching, tense, and more than a trifle discombobulated,[8] he still stood pressed into the shelter of a scrub pine as if it could hide him from her. "Are you caught by your mane or something?" Her hand groped, trying to ascertain that he was not. "I don't know a thing about horses," she confided.

Noooooo, no kidding. Even an ordinary farm horse had hooves that could trample her or kick her into next week, not to speak of inch-long chisel-like teeth that could sink into her. The Jersey Devil, being a meat eater, had even nastier teeth. Customized. *Want to see my fangs?* But he did not show them to her.

"Except that I read *The Black Stallion*," the girl added. "Can I ride you, black horse?" she asked wistfully.

Oh, for Heaven's sake . . .

He was already breaking all the rules. If a human did not run from his scream, he was supposed to rampage and snarl and glare and breathe fire until the human did run, and if those tactics failed, he was supposed to traumatize the human with his hooves. But poop on all that. Poop by the scoop. He just didn't feel like it.

Fine. Whatever.

He stepped away from the pine, arched his neck, and lowered his head in a fairy-tale gesture of equine acquiescence.[9] Apparently she knew

---

7 **extremity:** an extreme danger or need

8 **discombobulated:** confused; upset

9 **acquiescence:** consent; approval

enough about fairy tales, if not about horses, to recognize the body language. She immediately grabbed his mane and scrambled on. Those soft feet had usages after all. Her monkey toes dug into his foreleg and shoulder as she climbed him. Lightweight, she settled behind his withers,[10] her knees hooked around the junctures of his wings.

"Ooooh," she said, her voice worshipful and delighted, "it's high up here."

The Jersey Devil set off at a sullen, jarring walk, emerging from the pine scrub to plod down the berm[11] of the highway. So what if cars came by. So what if people saw him. His job description was ruined anyhow, and he wasn't sure what would happen to a minor monster who was doing some major messing up. His boss would have a few things to say, that was for sure.

"Oh, thank you," the girl said, though it was not clear for what she was thanking him, "thank you. Nobody else cares."

Shut up.

She did not shut up. "Nobody believes me, that's the problem," she said more softly. "Even my best girlfriend. Nobody wants to believe what's happening to me."

Like the girlfriend and the anonymous others, the Jersey Devil did not want to deal with it. *I've got my own problems.* He walked faster, slamming his heels into the ground with each step.

A mile passed, and another. Gradually his stride eased as the girl's warm presence massaged him. On his back she had gone into a trance of glory and was wordlessly singing. "I'll call you Blackie," she said suddenly. "No, that's stupid. I'll call you Black, uh, Black Angel." She said the name like an apotheosis.[12]

Up to this point the Jersey Devil had had only superficial experience of humans: Screech at them, and they ran. He had not had occasion to deal with the nearly religious fervor of a horse-besotted[13] girl. Her unquestioning adoration put him off balance.

"Where are we going?" she asked with utter faith.

Going? The Jersey Devil had not been thinking in terms of going anywhere. She wanted a horsie ride, and he was giving her a horsie ride. But

---

10 **withers:** area between the shoulder bones of a horse

11 **berm:** mound of earth; here, berm refers to the mound the highway is built upon

12 **apotheosis:** glorification; adoration

13 **besotted:** infatuated

now she had called him Black Angel, and she wanted to know where they were going—she expected him to take care of her? There was a large explosion in his small brain, expressed in a snort the size of the pine barrens, the original, not the remnants. Okay. Okay, he knew where they were going. They were going to get her something to eat, and they were going to plunge him all the way into deep manure. They were going somewhere he had never been in his entire three-hundred-year life.

They were going to McDonald's.

▲   ▲   ▲

His belly had been growling before they started, and it had become mighty in borborgymus[14] by the time they arrived at the golden arches. He saw at once that the puny doors were not large enough for him—too bad. Like a Mack truck going relentlessly into reverse, he backed up to the glass, feeling the girl grab his mane as she divined[15] his intentions; he kicked. She shrieked with glee as if on an amusement park ride. Other shrieks sounded from inside, not gleeful at all, and the Jersey Devil snorted with excitement, roused by the screams. He warmed to the sound of crashing, tinkling glass. As he continued to enlarge the entrance, the restaurant was emptying via the other doors. Cars zoomed from the parking lot, and he heard the girl on his back laughing. Such an intelligent child; she was not afraid. Not afraid at all.

He had opened almost the entire front of the establishment. There was no need for her to duck or risk her bare feet on broken glass as he carried her inside. Clear to the counter, where he stopped as if at a mounting block. She slipped down from his back to stand on the countertop, wobbling a little and hanging onto him until she got her legs back. "There's nobody to wait on us," she said, laughing.

The staff had disappeared from the kitchen area, as the Jersey Devil knew quite well; he had seen people in clownish uniforms running through the parking lot.

"I guess it's okay for me to help myself, since they ran away." She was serious now, wanting to know whether it was morally correct for her, a starving child, to take food, and she decided that since her guardian angel had brought her here, it had to be all right. "Are you hungry?" She dropped to her bony bottom and scooted down off the counter, heading

14 **borborgymus:** intestinal noises caused by moving gas
15 **divined:** predictied; understood

for where the paper-wrapped hamburgers were ranked on the rack underneath the heat lamp. She grabbed an armload of burgers, unwrapping several and spreading them on the counter in front of the Jersey Devil before she bit into one herself.

Ick. Cooked meat. No better than possum cooked in the sun for three days on an asphalt highway.

Still, the Jersey Devil ate. The bread was not too bad, though squashed. The dill pickle slices were interesting. But he soon diverted his attention from the burgers on the countertop to the leavings on the tables. There was a good grease smell emanating from many small cardboard containers, and thereby he discovered fries. Salty fries, he decided, are almost as good as fresh raw chicken with the feathers on. He munched them, cardboard and all. Behind the counter, the girl had gulped down three burgers and was holding her open mouth under the Coke spigot as she pushed the button.

In french fry gestalt,[16] the Jersey Devil only gradually became aware of an annoying noise: sirens. Louder, nearer. The next moment, several police cars screeched into the McDonald's parking lot.

With her bare feet making slapping noises on the floor, the girl came out from behind the counter, stood near the side door, and looked at the Jersey Devil as if awaiting directions. He was her bat-winged equine angel. She would do whatever he said.

Go away. Let me alone. He just wanted to eat fries. He was not afraid of the cops—their bullets could not so much as dent his black, supernatural hide. His fear was of other authorities.

The police had scurried and deployed themselves. McDonald's seemed to have a hot line straight to the precinct. "Come out with your hands up!" a cop barked into a megaphone.

If I come out with my hooves up, you're not going to like it, fella.

"Captain," one of the other cops yelled from near a side window, "I see him. Holy cow, it's some kind of big animal." The police officer, a youngster, maybe a rookie, began to shake as if with buck fever.[17] Having just discovered Chicken McNuggets en papier, the Jersey Devil did not even bother to glare as the young cop leveled his gun barrel and fired. Glass flew with a soprano song. The bullet ricocheted off the Jersey

---

16 **gestalt:** process whereby an individual takes in experience as a whole rather than in isolated parts; here, euphoria; happiness

17 **buck fever:** excitement of an inexperienced hunter when confronting game for the first time

Devil and shot harmlessly into a Ronald McDonald effigy[18] grinning in the corner, but the impact annoyed the Jersey Devil. He screeched and reared. Red lightning flashed in his eyes.

"Don't! Don't shoot at him; you'll hurt him!" The girl came running, placing her skinny body between the Jersey Devil and the offending cop.

Too late the Jersey Devil realized that although bullets could not kill him, they might very well kill her. He had to get her out of there.

It was a thought that upset the order of his universe, throwing a three-century lifetime's worth of assumptions into confusion. Not that confusion would not have existed anyway. There were shouts, another gunshot, yells—"Don't, idiot, you'll hit the kid!" He clattered across vinyl flooring and knocked tables cockeyed in his haste to stand by her, and she seemed to comprehend; she scrambled onto him. Her hand felt firm on his mane. She was okay so far.

He wheeled and leaped through the wide-open front entry. Instinctively, as whenever his adrenaline got going, his wings spread and beat the air. With his softly furred patagia[19] vibrating like drumheads, nearly singing, he surged upward. His forehooves struck the roof of the nearest cruiser; he tucked them and rose steeply, tidily clearing the ornamental pear trees.

"Oh," the girl squealed, "we're flying!"

She was not the only one who was impressed. The manly shoutings down below were achieving new heights of frenzy.

"Black Angel," the girl said, her voice hushed now, "this is wonderful. I've always wanted to fly."

Just hang on. If you splat, I'm not going to be the vulture that eats you.

The hoarse vociferations[20] of the police and onlookers faded away behind them. Flying at about five hundred feet over the lights of town, lugging a bit under the unaccustomed weight of a passenger, the Jersey Devil wheeled sluggishly southward toward the friendly darkness of the pine barrens. Now that his belly was approximately full, all he wanted was to get home, ditch this kid, and rest.

Sirens. Blue lights flashing on the roads below. The cops were following.

"Black Angel," the girl said with a panicky catch in her voice, "don't let them get me. Please don't. They'll send me back home . . ."

18 **effigy:** image or representation of a person

19 **patagia:** folds of skin near the front of a bird's wings

20 **vociferations:** yells, screams

It was the first time he had discerned fear in her. She was not afraid of him, a grotesque denizen of the night, yet she feared—who? what? It had to be a monster beyond imagining.

The police cruisers were following easily. Despite his bat wings, the Jersey Devil did not dart like a bat. Due to the bulk of his body, his air speed was modest, and he was too unwieldy to attempt sudden directional changes. Too bad. If he could swoop, maybe he could lose this kid.

"Please," she begged, her voice thin, terrified. "I can't go back there."

Of course, there were unquestionably ways he could get rid of her. All it would take would be a midair bucking spree—but even as he rather venomously thought that, he knew he was not going to do it.

"*Please,* Angel, do something."

I could bomb their windshields. But he knew that all the poop he had in him would not help for long. *All right, okay!* He did not like it, but he knew he would have to do it sooner or later anyway. Might as well take her with him. Maybe she could help plead his case.

To the watchers on the ground, looking up at his grotesque underbelly and wings and at the frail child riding him—"Write it up as a stranger abduction," the captain was telling the cop stuck with that unenviable job—to the watchers looking up at the bizarre horse-bat clearly visible in moonlight and in the light pollution from below, it was as if the apparition[21] vanished in midair, rider and all.

But to the Jersey Devil, a very minor nighttime manifestation in an unlikely place at an unsympathetic time, it was not that he had vanished. It was merely that, with a sigh and a sour-tempered rolling of his eyes, he had gone to face his tribunal.[22]

▲ ▲ ▲

This was not a nighttime place. This was a place where it was always light yet never light. A place forever dimly aglow in lambent[23] rainbow mist.

"Fool! Three-hundred-year upstart! A mere sprout! Who are you to dare to extemporize?"[24]

It was the World Tree who spoke, she whose crown was forever veiled in mist and mystery, she for whom "goddess" was too lowly a title. Even had the Jersey Devil not been kneeling before her, nose to the ground,

---

21 **apparition:** ghost; specter

22 **tribunal:** court, forum of justice

23 **lambent:** softly bright; radiant

24 **extemporize:** improvise; deviate from the plan

even had he been standing, he would have been able to see only the very least and lowest of her mighty branches stretching far overhead. Perching on the visible branches and looking down with a certain smug satisfaction (or so the Jersey Devil sensed) were various of the lesser mythical birds: the Gillygaloo (which laid cubical eggs and wept constantly), the lop-winged Whangdoodle, the backward Smollygaster, and many others, but no manifestations of any importance. Major mythological personages such as the Phoenix or the Roc would never be seen on such lowly branches; they were far overhead and out of sight, if indeed they were present at all. And the other winged beings, such as the Pegasus—of course they were far above, swaddled and haloed and glorified in fog. If the Pegasus were flying anywhere in the neighborhood, the Jersey Devil would never see him.

"Do you understand what you have done?" the World Tree continued to scold. "This girl, what are we to do with her? Now that she has seen us, she can never return."

"I don't want to return," the girl spoke up, her piping tone so brash in this empyrean[25] place that the Jersey Devil winced and trembled. "I don't care what happens to me. It can't be any worse than what has happened already."

"Nonsense. What can possibly be worse than exile from your people?"

The girl told her. As she spoke, and as the Jersey Devil began to comprehend, he felt an unfamiliar burning sensation within his chest, a hot pain that heaved his ribs, surged upward, and blocked his throat, stung his eyes. Without leave from the World Tree, he arose from his knees and went to the girl. What was this punishment taking hold of him, this saltwater tide of misery? His eyes were so blurred he could barely see the child as he reached out his gargoyle head to nuzzle her. The anguish ran out of his eyes and down his long, ugly face.

She turned to him and hugged him around his neck, hiding her face in his mane, and his tears dripped down on her back and shoulders. There was silence.

"Well . . . " the World Tree said at last, quite softly for such a presence.

The girl did not reply, but her head had lifted from the Jersey Devil's neck and behind her thick glasses her eyes were wide and shining. She gasped, "Wings!"

At the same time the Jersey Devil saw them budding, sprouting from her shoulders, pushing through the cloth of her cheap shirt—fabric wet from his tears—the way spring flowers push through last year's leaves. Wings worthy of a skylark. Airy, uplifted wings the color of raindrops.

Humbly the Jersey Devil turned to the World Tree and said it first. "Thank you, Mother."

"Nonsense. I gave her nothing. You gave them to her."

"I—I can fly?" stammered the girl. "Oh! Oh! Thank you! I've always wanted to fly." She jiggled, jumped, stood on tiptoes with arms outstretched.

"In a moment, little one. Patience. You, Black Thing, come here."

The Jersey Devil bowed his head and took a few steps forward. He sensed that it might be politic[26] to kneel again. But he did not.

"I am going to give you a change of assignment," said the World Tree.

---

25 **empyrean:** heavenly; ideal

26 **politic:** shrewdly tactful; expedient

"Decide for yourself whether it is an advancement or a demotion. I'll never tell."

It was hard to know how to react to the World Tree when she got that quirk in her voice. One did not quite dare to joke with her. The Jersey Devil said nothing.

"The pine barrens are a lost cause since the Turnpike went through," the World Tree said in resigned and contemplative tones. "Confine yourself to them no longer. Your new task is this: You are to seek out those who hurt children. By whatever means you choose, make their lives difficult. Do I make myself clear?"

The Jersey Devil's head had come up. His upper lip wrinkled in the equine equivalent of a smile. His fangs showed. He bowed low, then wheeled away, eager to get started.

"Little one," the World Tree concluded in bored tones, "you had better fly along with him to make sure he gets it right. He is rather stupid."

"All *right!*" The girl sprang into the timeless air. Her thin face grew rapt with the astonishment and glory of flying. Her glasses shone like the rainbow mist. "Come on, Black Angel!" she cried.

He leaped to fly beside her. When her wings grew tired, he would take her upon his back. He would soar smoothly so as not to joggle her, and perhaps she would lay her head on his neck and sleep.

My name is not Jersey Devil anymore.

Perhaps a monster, a devil, is not so far from being an angel. Perhaps the girl had named him rightly. Black Angel, Avenging Angel. What is an angel but a strange creature with wings?

▲ ▲ ▲

The Jersey Devil *is a holdover from an earlier era when the pine barrens of southern New Jersey were thinly populated and scary enough to support a supernatural manifestation. A horselike creature that was reputed to scream horribly in the barrens, leave hoofprints on housetops, kill chickens, and occasionally fly, the Jersey Devil might be a descendant of other horse-demons such as the Irish Pooka or whatever weird thing it was that left an arrow-straight line of hoofprints in fresh snow for ninety-seven miles along the South Devon coast in 1855.* ∾

The Wife's Story

Ursula K. Le Guin

He was a good husband, a good father. I don't understand it. I don't believe in it. I don't believe that it happened. I saw it happen but it isn't true. It can't be. He was always gentle. If you'd have seen him playing with the children, anybody who saw him with the children would have known that there wasn't any bad in him, not one mean bone. When I first met him he was still living with his mother over near Spring Lake, and I used to see them together, the mother and the sons, and think that any young fellow that was that nice with his family must be one worth knowing. Then one time when I was walking in the woods I met him by himself coming back from a hunting trip. He hadn't got any game at all, not so much as a field mouse, but he wasn't cast down about it. He was just larking¹ along enjoying the morning air. That's one of the things I first loved about him. He didn't take things hard, he didn't grouch and whine when things didn't go his way. So we got to talking that day. And I guess things moved right along after that, because pretty soon he was over here pretty near all the time. And my sister said—see, my parents had moved out the year before and gone South, leaving us the place—my sister said, kind of teasing but serious, "Well! If he's going to be here every day and half the night, I guess there isn't room for me!" And she moved out—just down the way. We've always been real close, her and me. That's the sort of thing doesn't ever change. I couldn't ever have got through this bad time without my sis.

---

1 **larking:** engaging in harmless fun or mischief

Well, so he came to live here. And all I can say is, it was the happiest year of my life. He was just purely good to me. A hard worker and never lazy, and so big and fine-looking. Everybody looked up to him, you know, young as he was. Lodge Meeting nights, more and more often they had him to lead the singing. He had such a beautiful voice, and he'd lead off strong, and the others following and joining in, high voices and low. It brings the shivers on me now to think of it, hearing it, nights when I'd stayed home from meeting when the children was babies—the singing coming up through the trees there, and the moonlight, summer nights, the full moon shining. I'll never hear anything so beautiful. I'll never know a joy like that again.

It was the moon, that's what they say. It's the moon's fault, and the blood. It was in his father's blood. I never knew his father, and now I wonder what become of him. He was from up Whitewater way, and had no kin around here. I always thought he went back there, but now I don't know. There was some talk about him, tales, that come out after what happened to my husband. It's something runs in the blood, they say, and it may never come out, but if it does, it's the change of the moon that does it. Always it happens in the dark of the moon. When everybody's home asleep. Something comes over the one that's got the curse in his blood, they say, and he gets up because he can't sleep, and goes out into the glaring sun, and goes off all alone—drawn to find those like him. And it may be so, because my husband would do that. I'd half rouse and say, "Where you going to?" and he'd say, "Oh, hunting, be back this evening," and it wasn't like him, even his voice was different. But I'd be so sleepy, and not wanting to wake the kids, and he was so good and responsible, it was no call of mine to go asking "Why?" and "Where?" and all like that.

So it happened that way maybe three times or four. He'd come back late, and worn out, and pretty near cross for one so sweet-tempered—not wanting to talk about it. I figured everybody got to bust out now and then, and nagging never helped anything. But it did begin to worry me. Not so much that he went, but that he come back so tired and strange. Even, he smelled strange. It made my hair stand up on end. I could not endure it and I said, "What is that—those smells on you? All over you!" And he said, "I don't know," real short, and made like he was sleeping. But he went down when he thought I wasn't noticing and washed and washed himself. But those smells stayed in his hair, and in our bed, for days.

And then the awful thing. I don't find it easy to tell about this. I want to cry when I have to bring it to my mind. Our youngest, the little one, my baby, she turned from her father. Just overnight. He come in and she got scared-looking, stiff, with her eyes wide, and then she begun to cry and try to hide behind me. She didn't yet talk plain but she was saying over and over, "Make it go away! Make it go away!"

The look in his eyes, just for one moment, when he heard that. That's what I don't want ever to remember. That's what I can't forget. The look in his eyes looking at his own child.

I said to the child, "Shame on you, what's got into you?"—scolding, but keeping her right up close to me at the same time, because I was frightened too. Frightened to shaking.

He looked away then and said something like, "Guess she just waked up dreaming," and passed it off that way. Or tried to. And so did I. And I got real mad with my baby when she kept on acting crazy scared of her own dad. But she couldn't help it and I couldn't change it.

He kept away that whole day. Because he knew, I guess. It was just beginning dark of the moon.

It was hot and close inside, and dark, and we'd all been asleep some while, when something woke me up. He wasn't there beside me. I heard a little stir in the passage, when I listened. So I got up, because I could bear it no longer. I went out into the passage, and it was light there, hard sunlight coming in from the door. And I saw him standing just outside, in the tall grass by the entrance. His head was hanging. Presently he sat down, like he felt weary, and looked down at his feet. I held still, inside, and watched—I didn't know what for.

And I saw what he saw. I saw the changing. In his feet, it was, first. They got long, each foot got longer, stretching out, the toes stretching out and the foot getting long, and fleshy, and white. And no hair on them.

The hair begun to come away all over his body. It was like his hair fried away in the sunlight and was gone. He was white all over, then, like a worm's skin. And he turned his face. It was changing while I looked. It got flatter and flatter, the mouth flat and wide, and the teeth grinning flat and dull, and the nose just a knob of flesh with nostril holes, and the ears gone, and the eyes gone blue—blue, with white rims around the blue—staring at me out of that flat, soft, white face.

He stood up then on two legs.

I saw him, I had to see him, my own dear love, turned into the hateful one.

I couldn't move, but as I crouched there in the passage staring out into the day I was trembling and shaking with a growl that burst out into a crazy, awful howling. A grief howl and a terror howl and a calling howl. And the others heard it, even sleeping, and woke up.

It stared and peered, that thing my husband had turned into, and shoved its face up to the entrance of our house. I was still bound by mortal fear, but behind me the children had waked up, and the baby was whimpering. The mother anger come into me then, and I snarled and crept forward.

The man thing looked around. It had no gun, like the ones from the man places do. But it picked up a heavy fallen tree-branch in its long white foot, and shoved the end of that down into our house, at me. I snapped the end of it in my teeth and started to force my way out, because I knew the man would kill our children if it could. But my sister was already coming. I saw her running at the man with her head low and her mane high and her eyes yellow as the winter sun. It turned on her and raised up that branch to hit her. But I come out of the doorway, mad with the mother anger, and the others all were coming answering my call, the whole pack gathering, there in that blind glare and heat of the sun at noon.

The man looked round at us and yelled out loud, and brandished the branch it held. Then it broke and ran, heading for the cleared fields and plowlands, down the mountainside. It ran, on two legs, leaping and weaving, and we followed it.

I was last, because love still bound the anger and the fear in me. I was running when I saw them pull it down. My sister's teeth were in its throat. I got there and it was dead. The others were drawing back from the kill, because of the taste of the blood, and the smell. The younger ones were cowering and some crying, and my sister rubbed her mouth against her forelegs over and over to get rid of the taste. I went up close because I thought if the thing was dead the spell, the curse must be done, and my husband could come back—alive, or even dead, if I could only see him, my true love, in his true form, beautiful. But only the dead man lay there white and bloody. We drew back and back from it, and turned and ran, back up into the hills, back to the woods of the shadows and the twilight and the blessed dark. ❧

Rikiki and the Wizard

A S'Rian Folk Story

Patricia C. Wrede

*O*nce there was a wizard whose luck time was three days long. He was the luckiest wizard in the world, and he worked hard at his magic. He did a good business working spells for the people of Liavek. But the wizard was not satisfied.

He bought himself musty dusty books in Old Tichenese and burned sheep-fat lamps until late at night while he read them and practiced the spells they contained. Soon he had a house on Wizards' Row, and the Levar himself was buying spells from him. But the wizard was not satisfied.

He traveled to faraway places to learn their magics, then went into his cellar and invented spells of his own. He became the best wizard in the world, as well as the luckiest. People came from Ka Zhir and Tichen and even from the Farlands just to buy spells from him. The wizard became very rich and very famous. But he was still not satisfied.

"Everyone knows who I am now," he said to himself. "But in a few hundred years they will not remember me. I must find a way to make my reputation last."

Now, the wizard had a daughter of whom he was very proud. She had skin like a flower petal, and long hair that fell down to her feet, and bright black eyes that danced like the sun on the Sea of Luck. She was the most beautiful woman in seven cities, and her name was Ryvenna.

The wizard decided to call on the gods and offer his daughter in marriage to whichever one would promise to make him so rich and so

THE ASTROLOGER
1916
N.C. Wyeth

famous that he would never be forgotten for as long as people lived around the Sea of Luck. "For," he thought, "not only will I be as rich and famous as anyone could desire, I will also get my Ryvenna a husband worthy of her beauty."

The wizard made his preparations and cast his spells. He worked for a week to get everything right. But the gods were angry with him, because he had never asked his daughter whether she agreed to his plan.

"Bad enough that he presumes we'd want her," grumbled Welenen the Rain-Bringer. "But giving the girl away without telling her? He acts as if she were a pet dog or a camel!" And the other gods agreed.

So when the wizard cast his spell, none of the gods would answer. He called and called, for two days and for three days, and nothing happened. Finally he resolved to try one last time. He set out the gold wire and burned the last of the special herbs and put all of his luck into the spell (and he was the luckiest wizard in the world).

Now, Rikiki had been at the meeting where all the gods agreed not to answer the wizard's summons, and he had agreed with them. But Rikiki is a blue chipmunk, and chipmunks do not have long memories. Furthermore, they are insatiably curious. When the wizard put all his effort into his last try, Rikiki couldn't resist answering, just to see what was happening. So when the smoke cleared, the wizard saw a blue chipmunk sitting before him, looking up at him with black eyes. "Nuts?" asked Rikiki.

The wizard was very angry to find that the only god who had answered his summons was a blue chipmunk. But Rikiki *was* a god, so the wizard said, "Rikiki! I will give you my daughter, who is the most beautiful woman in seven cities, if you will make me as rich and famous as I desire!"

"Daughter?" said Rikiki, "What daughter? New kind of nut?"

"No. She is a woman, the most beautiful woman in seven cities, and I will give her to you if you do as I ask!"

"Oh!" said Rikiki. "Seven cities of nuts! What want?"

"No, no! My daughter, not nuts!"

"Daughter? Don't want daughter. Want nuts! Where nuts?"

By this time, the wizard had decided that Rikiki was no use to him, so he said, "North, Rikiki. North along the shore of the Sea of Luck. Lots of nuts, Rikiki!"

"Good!" said Rikiki. "Like nuts!" And he scurried out of the wizard's house and ran north. He ran up and down the shore of the Sea of Luck, looking for the nuts the wizard had promised, but he didn't find any. He dug holes in the ground, looking for the nuts. The dirt that he threw out of the holes became the Silverspine Mountains, but Rikiki didn't find any nuts. So he went back to the wizard's house.

"No nuts north!" said Rikiki. "Where nuts?"

"I don't have any nuts!" said the wizard. "Go away!"

"Said nuts north. Didn't find nuts. Want nuts! Where look?"

"Go west, Rikiki," said the wizard. "Go a long, long way. Find nuts. And don't come back!"

"Good!" said Rikiki. "Like nuts!" And he scurried out of the wizard's house and ran west. He ran for a long, long time, but he didn't find any nuts. Finally he came to a mountain range on the other side of the plains. "No nuts here," said Rikiki, and he turned around and went back. It was midday and the sun was very hot. Rikiki let his tail droop on the ground as he ran, and it made a line in the dusty ground. The line became the Cat River. But Rikiki still didn't find any nuts. So he went to see the wizard again.

"No nuts west!" Rikiki said when he got back to the wizard's house. "Where nuts?"

"Not again!" said the wizard.

"Want nuts!" Rikiki insisted. He looked at the wizard with his black eyes.

The wizard remembered that Rikiki was a god, and he began to be a little frightened. "No nuts here, Rikiki," he said.

"Promised nuts!" said Rikiki. "Where?"

The wizard thought for a moment, then he said, "Go south, Rikiki. Go a long, long way south." He knew that south of Liavek is the Sea of Luck, and he was sure that it was deep enough and wide enough to drown a chipmunk, even if the chipmunk was a god.

Rikiki nodded and scurried off. The wizard heaved a sigh of relief and sat down to think of some other way to become rich and famous forever.

Now, the wizard's daughter Ryvenna had been listening at the door since her father started his spell casting. She had thought Rikiki sounded nice, so she ran out to the Two-Copper Bazaar and bought some chestnuts from a street vendor. She returned just in time to hear the wizard send Rikiki south to drown in the Sea of Luck.

Quickly, Ryvenna opened up the bag of chestnuts. When Rikiki came scurrying out, she said, "Nuts, Rikiki! Here are nuts!" and held out the bag.

Rikiki stopped. "Nuts? Nuts for Rikiki?" He came over and sat in Ryvenna's lap while she fed him all the chestnuts she had brought from the Two-Copper Bazaar. When he finished, he looked up and said hopefully, "Nice nut lady! More nuts?"

"I'm sorry, Rikiki," said Ryvenna. "They're all gone."

"Oh! Fix easy," said Rikiki. He looked at the empty bag and crossed his eyes, and the bag was full again. "More nuts!" he said, and Ryvenna fed him again.

Rikiki was finishing the second bag of nuts when the wizard came out of his study. "What is he doing here?" the wizard demanded when he saw Rikiki.

"Eating nuts," said his daughter coolly. She was annoyed with him for trying to marry her to a god without asking her, and for trying to drown Rikiki. "He made the bag fill up again after it was empty."

"I don't care about nuts!" said the wizard.

Rikiki looked up. "Not like nuts?"

"Nuts aren't worth anything for people! I want gold! I want to be famous! And I want that blue chipmunk out of my house!"

"Oh!" said Rikiki. He looked cross-eyed at the bag again, then said to Ryvenna, "Dump over."

Ryvenna turned the bag upside down. A stream of gold chestnuts fell out, more chestnuts than the bag could possibly hold. They rolled all over the floor. The wizard stood staring with his mouth open.

"Gold nuts for nice nut lady!" said Rikiki happily. The wizard closed his mouth and swallowed twice. Then he said, "What about my fame?"

"Fame?" said Rikiki. "What fame? Fame good to eat? Like nuts?"

"No, Rikiki," Ryvenna said. "Fame is having everyone know who you are. Father wants to be so famous no one will ever forget him."

"Oh!" Rikiki thought for minute. "Not forget?"

"That's right!" said the wizard eagerly.

Rikiki sat very still, staring at the wizard, and his tail twitched. Then he said, "Not forget! All fixed."

"You have?" said the wizard, who was beginning to regret sending Rikiki to drown in the Sea of Luck.

"All done," Rikiki replied. He looked at Ryvenna. "Nuts all gone. 'Bye, nice nut lady!" And he disappeared.

"Well," said the wizard, "there's the last of my wishes; that blasted blue chipmunk is gone."

"I thought he was cute," said Ryvenna.

"Bah! He's a silly blue god who'll do anything for nuts. It was very clever of you to get some for him. Now help me pick up these gold chestnuts he made for me; we wouldn't want to lose one."

The wizard bent over and tried to pick up one of the golden chestnuts, but as soon as he touched it, it turned into a real chestnut. He threw it down and tried another, but the same thing happened. Only Ryvenna could pick up the golden chestnuts without changing them back into real ones, and the magic chestnut bag would only make more gold for her. Worse yet, the wizard discovered that whenever he touched one of his gold levars it, too, turned into a chestnut. So did his jeweled belts and bracelets. Even the food he ate turned into chestnuts as soon as he touched it.

The wizard tried to keep his affliction[1] a secret, but it was impossible. Soon everyone was talking about what Rikiki had done to the luckiest wizard in the world. Even people who never bought spells and who had no dealings with magicians heard the story and laughed at it. So the wizard became more famous than ever, more famous, indeed, than he wanted to be. And his fame has lasted to this day, for people still tell his story.

Ryvenna was a clever woman, and she knew that magic does not last. The magic chestnut bag ran out in a year and a day, but before it did she had poured a goodly supply of gold chestnuts from it. She became a wealthy woman, and eventually fell in love with and married a sea captain who was as kind as he was handsome. And she never forgot to leave a bowl of nuts at the door for Rikiki every night as long as she lived. ∾

---

1 **affliction:** curse; suffering

The Stone Girl

Elise Matthesen

She wasn't a stone girl at first, of course. Even after she was, it wasn't something as you would notice right off. I came after it happened, so there wasn't any "befores" for me to be comparing, but her sister said there wasn't much change to look at. Just one day to the next her skin getting colder, a little more solid.

I came when her sister finally allowed that she needed help with the work around the place. The stone girl still moved then, though she was slow. Deliberate, like she had to think where her arm should be next. Wasn't much could be done by her in the way of chores. She had told her sister this, the words coming one by one, dropping like pebbles in a pond. The sister asked in town the next day for help. I came directly; there wasn't anything that greatly held me to the place I had been. Truth be told, I wasn't much the kind that could be held. So I came, and if I wasn't expecting anything fine, well, then, I wasn't likely to be disappointed. That was how I figured. But they had a welcome for me, and a place prepared. They treated me nice, too, the sisters; I had a feathertick[1] fine as theirs, and we ate from the same kettle. The feathertick I pulled into the sleeping porch after the first few nights, seeing as it was a warm spring. That way I could be up and about in the mornings without having to go through and wake them. I didn't know for sure if the stone girl slept or not, but her sister I expected could use any rest that was offered her.

I asked early what the cause for all this might have been. It's not something I had ever heard tell of before, even living on the edge of the Marshes. The sister told me that one day the stone girl had come back to the house shivering and shaken. She hadn't been able to tell her sister

---

1 **feathertick:** mattress filled with feathers

much, just that she had gotten tangled in some spellweb. Or maybe it was some bargain made by an old marsh wisewit that maybe didn't get paid off at the time and just sort of hung there until it caught the sleeve of the next person walking by. The stone girl didn't know, and her sister, though she studied on it, couldn't bring a better guess to it. Anywise, the sense and direction of it was clear: it was a Change Spell. What came was stone; what went was flesh. Or at least touch, warmth, receiving and reaching out. Those were flesh things.

That was why the lover left, the sister told me. He wept some and raged against the Marshes and against spellpowers in general and wise-wits in particular, and he came and sat with the stone girl on the front stairs. After a while he came to realize that she couldn't feel it when he clasped her hand and complained over the unkindness of fate. Not too long after that he was walking out with another young woman. I saw them once when I was pulling Annie-go-courting[2] for the dyepot. They were careful not to walk out toward the Marshes, though, so I hadn't seen them after that. The sister was with me that one time, and I saw her turn her head until they were past.

"Maybe she don't feel it," she said, "but I do." I didn't ask her what she meant.

The once that I asked, the sister told me that the stone girl knew what was going to happen to her. Said she felt it somewhere inside, all wrote out like a book, only she didn't know the words for the whole of it. Maybe she did, and her sister was just chary[3] of relating it; it's not something I can know. Anywise, they're entitled to some secrets between them, if that's the way of it. What she did tell me was this: The stone girl would change, stone for flesh, until all of her was gone except the heart. Then when she died, her heart would turn into a beautiful bird and rise up singing. When the sister told me that, I tried to imagine such a bird. Maybe all of jewel colors, or red like the sun through the morning clouds.

"It might not be too long," she told me, "but even if it is, I'm bound to stay. She was proud, wouldn't beg me for it, but I know she wanted it. Wanted me to promise I'd stay and wait for that bird." She was silent for a stretch. "Ought to be some rare sight, that bird." We both of us sat awhile, looking at the clouds leaking color from the sun behind them. She made a little sound like the way the wind moves the rushgrass, and then we sat some more.

2 **Annie-go-courting:** name of a plant used to make dye

3 **chary:** cautious; wary

I was kind as I knew how to be with the stone girl, but it wasn't a thing that was easy. One day I felt a breeze coming up from the pond, and I went to put a big soft shawl around her. It was a thick patterned thing all in colors like the hues of marshflowers. The sister had made it. I had it mostly tucked in before it came to me that the stone girl probably couldn't feel it anyway. Neither shawl nor breeze, come to that. I stood there like a post for a bit, thinking, until the sister came into the room and caught me at it. Might be that my thoughts were writ large[4] on my face, or maybe the sister had the advantage of having gone over the same ground herself. Anywise, she knew what I was coming to understand, and how I felt about it. I let her draw me away and back onto the porch, and I let her tell me.

She said she expected I was right about the stone girl not being able to feel much any more, but she had thought this out and come to a resting place with it. "Maybe she's in there, feeling everything, and just can't speak of it to us. I'd rather we took the chance and offered comfort to her. I think she knows; she can still see and hear us some, I expect. And even if she can't feel it, it makes me no matter. It's still comfort to me." And after thinking on it I came to decide that she was right.

I was out on the steps of an evening counting stars when I heard the sister's loom stop. Her footsteps moved across to the stone girl's chair and then fell quiet. There was a moan like November wind, and a thump. I looked in to see the sister kneeling against the stone girl's chair, hugging her and weeping.

She looked up at me when I poked my head in. "I felt her Change," she said.

I looked at the stone girl. Her mouth was a little open, like she had been trying to say something.

"Is she dead?" I asked, coming into the circle of firelight.

"No," her sister said, continuing to stroke the unresponsive arm. "No. She's not quite to the other bank of the water yet." And she sat there, keeping vigil,[5] with her eyes clear and the tears falling like spring rain.

I went out on the steps again. The stars were still there. I sat and thought about birds with wings all of jewels and fire.

It ought to be a rare sight. I expect I'll stay and be witness to it. ❧

4 **writ large:** clearly or freely written

5 **vigil:** watch

Between the Lines

RUTH TROWBRIDGE

Don't tell me again that one day
Prince Charming will arrive.
I remember all those fairy tales—
Only too well.
Who could take seriously
Some guy who'd spend half his life
Searching for thornless roses in the Snow?
Or traveling east of the sun and west of the moon?
Or trying to climb glass mountains?
His reward is to marry the fair princess
(Whose opinion is never asked)
And live happily ever after.
But what about the princess?
What's her reward?
He gets to quaff mead[1] with his cronies,
Open Parliament,
And show everyone the picture of him
Standing on the dragon's head.
She gets to keep a drafty castle clean,
Plan the banquets,
Have the babies,
And keep from screaming every time someone says,
"Is your husband *the* Prince Charming?
You lucky girl!"
Personally, I'd rather wait for Rumpelstiltskin,
At least, he'll expect me to think.

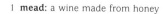

1 **mead:** a wine made from honey

RESPONDING TO CLUSTER FOUR

THINKING ON YOUR OWN
Thinking Skill SYNTHESIZING

1. Each of the other clusters in this book is introduced by a question that is meant to help readers focus their thinking about the selections. What do you think the question for Cluster Four should be?

2. How do you think the selections in this cluster should be taught? Demonstrate your ideas by joining with your classmates to: create discussion questions, lead discussions about the selections, develop vocabulary activities, and/or prepare a cluster quiz.

REFLECTING ON *FLIGHTS OF FANTASY*
Essential Question WHY READ FANTASY?

Reflecting on this book as a whole provides an opportunity for independent learning and the application of the critical thinking skill called synthesis. *Synthesizing* means examining all the things you have learned from this book and combining them to form a greater understanding of the difference between reality and fantasy and the appeal of fantasy fiction.

1. After reading this book you should have a better idea of the broad range of fantasy literature. You should also have some well-formed positions on your reading preferences regarding this genre. As you read, your position may have changed from positive to negative or vice versa. Write an essay that states your opinion about reading fantasy. Start with an opinion statement such as "Reading fantasy fiction is _____. (silly, fun, a waste of time, a great escape, fascinating, boring, etc). Back up your opinion with reasons that explain why you feel as you do.

2. It is estimated that a child will watch 8000 murders on TV before finishing elementary school and by age 18 will witness 200,000 acts of television violence. Some people argue that this kind of media barrage plus video games, movies, song lyrics, and so forth have blurred the lines between fantasy and reality for young people. Stage a debate in your class on the following issue.

   Resolved: Media violence destroys the ability to distinguish between fantasy and reality.

3. Individually or in small groups, develop an independent project that demonstrates your knowledge of and ideas about fantasy. Options might include research, music, dance, poetry, drama, original art, creating a fantasy art gallery, building a mini-library of fantasy favorites, or writing and reading aloud your own fantasy literature.

AUTHOR BIOGRAPHIES

ISAAC ASIMOV It would be hard to imagine a writer more prolific than Isaac Asimov. In his 72 years, he wrote or edited more than 500 books. Though he is best known for his science-fiction novels, he wrote on other subjects as well; his writings are classified in every library subject area except philosophy. Born in Russia in 1920, Asimov and his family immigrated to the United States when he was three years old. They opened a candy store, where young Asimov worked and read the science-fiction magazines that were for sale. He began writing at the age of eleven, and by the time he was eighteen, he had sold his first story. As an adult, Asimov earned a Ph.D. in chemistry from Columbia University, then worked as a chemist at Boston University until writing took his full attention. He also served as president of the American Humanist Society from 1985 until his death in 1992. His science-fiction novels, many which explain difficult concepts in simple ways, are among the most popular books ever written in that genre. Along with Robert Heinlein and Arthur C. Clarke, Asimov is considered one of the three "masters" of science-fiction writing.

ORSON SCOTT CARD Known primarily as the writer of the science fiction/fantasy Ender series (*Ender's Game* and *Ender's Shadow* among them), Orson Scott Card also writes biblical novels (such as *Sarah* from the Women of Genesis series), poetry, and plays. He also maintains a Web site featuring writing advice, weekly columns, social commentary, and reviews. Though he writes in a variety of literary styles, Card always emphasizes moral issues. Card, who has won both Hugo and Nebula awards, recently accepted a permanent appointment as a professor at Southern Virginia University.

WIM COLEMAN A prolific writer on a variety of subjects, Wim Coleman has been collaborating for over twenty years with his wife Pat Perrin. Some of their books are published under the pseudonym Cole Perriman. Coleman writes in many genres but he may be best known as a playwright; his plays have been produced throughout the United States, and several have won awards. In 2005, Coleman published the first book in a new fantasy series based on myths and legends. He is the author of Perfection Learning's *Stages of History* and *Nine Muses* collections. Coleman and Perrin live in San Miguel de Allende, Mexico, where they are helping raise a seven-year-old girl.

JOHN COLLIER was born in London in 1901 and published his first poem in 1920. He began his career writing poems, short stories, and novels, and many of his short stories were published by *The New Yorker*. In 1935, he moved to Hollywood and began writing television scripts and screenplays, including several scripts for *Alfred Hitchcock Presents*. During the 1950s, Collier won the Edgar Allan Poe Award and the Hugo Award. Collier died in 1980. Despite his literary prizes and commercial success, he never found literary acclaim. For many years, his works were out of print. Nevertheless, fantasy buffs extolled his stories, and some of them have recently been reprinted.

Jim Cort lives in New Jersey with his wife and family of three girls, one guinea pig, two dogs, and two cats. He writes short stories, nonfiction, and radio scripts, many of which can be downloaded from the Internet. Cort travels his home state giving talks on "The War of the Worlds," the 1938 radio broadcast by Orson Welles that alarmed listeners by reporting that a "huge flaming object" had dropped on a farm near Grovers Mill, New Jersey. His favorite medium is radio.

Peter Dickinson Declaring that he never *became* a writer, Peter Dickinson maintains that he has *been* a writer for as long as he can remember. He describes himself on his Web site as a tall, elderly, bony, beaky, wrinkled sort of fellow with a lot of untidy grey hair and a weird hooting voice. Dickinson was born in central Africa and raised mostly in England. After graduating from Cambridge University, he served in the British army and then worked for *Punch* magazine for seventeen years. Dickinson tried his hand, unsuccessfully, at writing a murder mystery before turning to fantasy. He has since written more than 50 books and has collaborated with his wife, Robin McKinley, on a collection of tales linked by an aquatic theme, called *Water: Tales of Elemental Spirits*. Dickinson, who writes for both juveniles and adults, has won many awards, including the Carnegie Medal and the Whitbread Children's Award.

Lord Dunsany Born in 1878, Edward John Moreton Drax Plunkett became the eighteenth Baron Dunsany in 1899. Dunsany served in the Boer War and World War I before settling in at Dunsany Castle in Meath, Ireland. He paid to have his first book of fantasy published in 1905, but he went on to become one of the most influential writers ever to write fantasy literature. Almost everything Dunsany wrote has been acclaimed, but his best-loved works are the fantasy stories he produced between 1905 and 1911 and the stage plays he produced until his death in 1957. "Idle Days on the Yann" and "A Shop in Go-by Street" are but two of his much-loved tales.

Betsy Hearne In addition to being a poet, Betsy Hearne is a professor of children's literature and storytelling at the University of Illinois graduate school of library science. Several of her books for children have won awards, including the 1998 Jane Addams Children's Book Award for *Seven Brave Women* and a Parents' Choice Silver Honor Award. Hearne has worked for more than 30 years as a book editor and reviewer and still writes reviews for the *New York Times Book Review*.

Marvin Kaye is the author of more than twenty books and a contributor to dozens more. He has also written several plays and dramatic adaptations of works and is the editor of both *H.P. Lovecraft's Magazine of Horror* and *Sherlock Holmes Mystery Magazine*. In addition to writing and editing literature, he promotes it as well. Kaye is on staff at Mercy College in Manhattan, where he directs its tutoring program, and he is an adjunct professor of creative writing at NYU.

URSULA K. LE GUIN When it comes to writing, Ursula K. Le Guin can do almost anything. She has published six books of poetry, several books of children's fiction, twenty novels, and more than a hundred short stories. She has also published books of essays as well as the translated works of other authors. Her writing has repeatedly won awards such as the National Book Award, the Pushcart Prize, the Hugo Award, and the Nebula Award, among others. Le Guin's best-known books are those in the Earthsea Trilogy, which have been translated into sixteen languages. Though she was born and grew up in Berkeley, California, Le Guin has lived in Portland, Oregon, since 1958, where she protects her private life but occasionally offers writing workshops.

ELISE MATTHESEN is a writer, speaker, workshop presenter, and jewelry maker whose nickname is Lioness. She is an active participant in the Artist's Challenge, a project in which artists create works in one medium that are inspired by the work of artists in another medium.

TAMORA PIERCE Born to a poor family in rural Pennsylvania in 1954, Tamora Pierce grew up telling herself stories about girl warriors. She credits her father with suggesting she write these stories down. Pierce wrote her first novel after graduating from college. It was never published—until a friend and literary agent at the agency where she worked suggested she carve her long novel into four young-adult fantasy novels. These books—the Circle of Magic series—launched Pierce's writing career. In 1991, Pierce began to support herself by writing. She has published many fantasy books for young readers and edited, with Josepha Sherman, the anthology *Young Warriors: Stories of Strength*. She continues to specialize in heroines she describes as "girls who kick butt."

NEAL SHUSTERMAN Born and raised in Brooklyn, New York, Neal Shusterman began writing stories in ninth grade when a teacher offered him extra credit for writing a story a month. Shortly after he graduated from college, he began writing a humor column that was picked up by the Syndicated Writer's Group. Since that time, he has also found success as a novelist, screenwriter, and television writer. Shusterman also has created mystery games for teens and adults. He has won dozens of awards for his work, including several American Library Association awards. Currently, he lives in California with his four children, whom he describes as a "constant inspiration."

STEVIE SMITH Born in England in 1903, Stevie Smith's father abandoned the family when she was just three, forcing Smith, her mother, and her sister to move in with an aunt. Smith contracted tuberculosis at age five and was sent away to live in a sanitarium for several years. Upon her recovery, she returned to her aunt's home, where she lived the rest of her life. Because she did not want to become a teacher, Smith attended secretarial school and took a job as a private secretary, writing in her free time. In 1936, she published a well-received novel, and the next year she published her first volume of poems. In 1953, Smith quit her job and began to write full-time. Eventually, she produced three novels and nine volumes of poetry, which she often illustrated with small sketches. Gradually, both her writing and her sketches found admirers, especially among younger readers. By the time she died in 1971, Smith's work was both well-known and widely admired.

NANCY SPRINGER   A versatile writer of fiction, nonfiction, short stories, and poetry for children and young adults, Nancy Springer has won more than a dozen awards for her work. She is best known as a fantasy writer, but she also teaches creative writing at York College in Pennsylvania and visits elementary, middle, and high schools to facilitate writing workshops for kids. When she is not writing, teaching writing, or promoting writing, Springer volunteers at the Wind Ridge Farm Equine Sanctuary and at Animal Rescue, Inc.

LOUIS UNTERMEYER   Although he was an accomplished poet, writer, editor, anthologist, translator, and lecturer, Louis Untermeyer never finished high school. He was born in New York City in 1885, and like many young men of his time, he quit school to work for his father as a jewelry manufacturer. Yet he couldn't resist writing. In 1911, Untermeyer published his first book of poems, *First Love*. Soon after, he and other left-leaning writers began publishing a Marxist journal, *The Masses*, which argued against U.S. involvement in World War I. After the United States entered the war, the government forced the magazine out of business. Not to be deterred, Untermeyer and friends launched a new magazine called the *Liberator*. In 1923, Untermeyer quit working in his father's company and devoted himself full-time to literature. He continued working for leftist causes and during the McCarthy era was blacklisted. In 1956, however, he won a gold medal from the Poetry Society of America. Shortly afterward, he became a poetry consultant for the Library of Congress. Louis Untermeyer died in 1977.

PATRICIA C. WREDE was born in Chicago, Illinois, in 1953. She attended college and graduate school in Minnesota, where she still lives. Though she was already writing when she was in seventh grade, Wrede began her career in the field of finance. She wrote fantasy stories and retellings of fairy tales on her own time, publishing four novels before deciding to quit her job and write full-time. Wrede has created three distinct fantasy series, several individual novels, countless short stories, and two collaborative novels. She also has contributed to the *Star Wars* novelization series.

ADDITIONAL READING

Abarat, Clive Barker. Candy Quackenbush of Chickentown, Minnesota, one day finds herself on the edge of a foreign world that is populated by strange creatures, and her life is forever changed. (c)2002

An Acceptable Time, Madeleine L'Engle. In this enthralling tale of time travel, Polly is swept from her grandparents' farm back to a world 3,000 years ago and comes face-to-face with a fierce people who believe in human sacrifice. (c)1990

Across the Nightingale Floor: Tales of the Otori, Book One, Lian Hearn. In his black-walled fortress at Inuyama, the warlord Lida Sadamu surveys his famous nightingale floor. Constructed with exquisite skill, it sings at the tread of each human foot. No assassin can cross it. (c)2003

The Dark Is Rising, Susan Cooper. For the twelve days of Christmas, life for Will Stanton is simultaneously ordinary and wonderful as he is drawn through terror and delight into the eternal conflict between good and evil. Newbery Honor winner. (c)1999

Dealing with Dragons, Patricia C. Wrede. Cimorene, the daughter of a very proper king, runs away and becomes the princess of the very powerful dragon, Kazul. Enchanted Forest Chronicles #1. (c)1996

Dragonflight, Anne McCaffrey. Adventures of the magnificent flying Dragonriders of Pern. (c)1986

Dragon of the Lost Sea, Laurence Yep. Shimmer, a renegade dragon princess, tries to redeem herself by capturing a witch with the help of a human boy. (c)1988

Dragon Rider, Cornelia Funke. After learning that humans are headed toward his hidden home, Firedrake, a silver dragon, is joined by a brownie and an orphan boy in a quest to find the legendary valley known as the Rim of Heaven. They encounter friendly and unfriendly creatures along the way and struggle to evade the relentless pursuit of an old enemy. (c)2004

East, Edith Pattou. A young woman journeys to a distant castle on the back of a great white bear who is the victim of a cruel enchantment. (c)2003

The Goblin Wood, Hilari Bell. A young Hedgewitch, an idealistic knight, and an army of clever goblins fight against the ruling hierarchy that is trying to rid the land of all magical creatures. (c)2003

Grass for His Pillow: Tales of the Otori, Book Two, Lian Hearn. The story of Takeo, the young orphan taken up by the Otori Lord and now a closely held member of the Tribe, and his beloved Shirakawa Kaede, heir to the Maruyama, who must find a way to unify the domain she has inherited. (c)2003

The Hero and the Crown, Robin McKinley. Fighting the dragon made girl-warrior Aerin a legend for all time and a true hero who would wield the power of the blue sword. Sequel to *The Blue Sword*. Newbery Medal winner. (c)1987

A Hidden Magic, Vivian Vande Velde. Fantasy parody about a plain princess and a reluctant wizard who must save a conceited prince who has offended a witch. (c)1997

The Hobbit, J.R.R. Tolkien. This stirring adventure is a fantasy that introduces the far-wandering hobbit, Bilbo Baggins. (c)1982

King of Shadows, Susan Cooper. While in London as part of an all-boy acting company preparing to perform in a replica of the famous Globe Theatre, Nat Field suddenly finds himself transported back to 1599 and performing in the original theater under the tutelage of Shakespeare himself. (c)1999

King of the Middle March, Kevin Crossley-Holland. As Arthur waits for the start of the fourth Crusade, when his future should be clearest, he feels the most doubt. Jealousies and greed rive the Crusade, leading him to question its true mission. And his seeing stone shows him the last days of King Arthur's court—a great dream destroyed, but also a glorious legend rising from the ruins. (c)2004

The Lion, the Witch and the Wardrobe, C.S. Lewis. First in the famous Chronicles of Narnia series. (c)

Loamhedge, Brian Jacques. While a group of adventurers from Redwall seeks out the ancient abbey of Loamhedge in hopes of curing a young haremaid's paralysis, Redwall is besieged by vermin. Number 16 in the Redwall Chronicles. (c)2003

Redwall, Brian Jacques. In the glorious tradition of *Watership Down* comes the heart-soaring story of a wondrous quest to recover a legendary lost weapon and a bumbling young apprentice monk named Matthias, mousekind's most unlikely hero. First in the Redwall Chronicles. (c)1990

The Remarkable Journey of Prince Jen, Lloyd Alexander. Bearing six unusual gifts, young Prince Jen embarks on a perilous quest and triumphantly enters into manhood. (c)1993

The Seeing Stone, Kevin Crossley-Holland. In late twelfth-century England, a thirteen-year-old boy named Arthur recounts how Merlin gives him a magical seeing stone, which shows him images of the legendary King Arthur, whose life seems to parallel his own. (c)2001

Seventh Son, Orson Scott Card. In an alternate early nineteenth-century America where folk magic works, Alvin Miller is born the seventh son of a seventh son, capable of powerful magic. First in the Tales of Alvin Maker series. (c)1988

Shadowmancer, G.P. Taylor. When Obadiah Demurral, the power-hungry Vicar of Thorpe, attempts to become a god by dabbling in magic, Raphah joins forces with Kate and Thomas to stop him. (c)2003

The Tale of Despereaux: Being the Story of a Mouse, a Princess, Some Soup, and a Spool of Thread, Kate DiCamillo. The adventures of Despereaux Tilling, a small mouse of unusual talents, the princess that he loves, the servant girl who longs to be a princess, and a devious rat determined to bring them all to ruin. Newbery Medal winner. (c)2003

The Treekeepers, Susan Britton. Searching for her father, Bird joins three other children, Issie, Dren, and Stoke, on a journey to the Kingdom of Wen to overthrow the evil Lord Rendarren. (c)2003

Watership Down, Richard Adams. The unique odyssey of a rabbit warren and their efforts to survive when a construction team moves into their territory. (c)1975

The Wee Free Men, Terry Pratchett. Tiffany, a young witch-to-be in the land of Discworld, teams up with the Wee Free Men, a clan of six-inch-high blue men, to rescue her baby brother and ward off a sinister invasion from Fairyland. (c)2001

A Wizard of Earthsea, Ursula K. Le Guin. Ged, the boy wizard, brings forth a beast that wants to destroy his soul. First of the Earthsea Trilogy. (c)1975

Acknowledgments

Text Credits CONTINUED FROM PAGE 2   "Middle Woman" by Orson Scott Card. Copyright © 1981 by Orson Scott Card. Reprinted by permission of The Barbara Bova Literary Agency.

"Ms. Lipshutz and the Goblin" by Marvin Kaye. Copyright © 1979, 1981 by Marvin Kaye. All rights reserved. Reprinted by permission of the author's agents, Donald Maass Literary Agency, 157 West 57th Street, Suite 703, New York, NY 10019.

"Plain Magic" by Tamora Pierce. Copyright © 1986, 1999 by Tamora Pierce. First published in slightly different form in *Planetfall*, Douglas Hill, editor; Oxford University Press U. K. Reprinted by permission of Harold Ober Associates Incorporated.

"Rikiki and the Wizard" by Patricia C. Wrede from Book of Enchantments. Copyright © 1986 by Patricia C. Wrede; originally published in *Liavek: The Players of Luck* (Berkley Publishing) edited by Will Shetterly and Emma Bull. Reprinted by permission of the author and her agent, Valerie Smith Literary Agency.

"Sir Gawain and the Loathly Lady," story adapted by Joanna Hearne from "The Weddynge of Sir Gawen and Dame Ragnell." Reprinted from *Beauties & Beasts: The Oryx Multicultural Folktale Series*, by Betsy Hearne. Copyright © 1993 by The Oryx Press. Used with permission from the author and The Oryx Press, 4041 N. Central Ave., Suite 700, Phoenix, AZ, 85012. 800-279-6799. http://www.oryxpress.com.

"The Spring" from *The Lion Tamer's Daughter and Other Stories* by Peter Dickinson. Copyright © 1997 by Peter Dickinson. Used by permission of Random House Children's Books, a division of Random House, Inc.

"The Stone Girl" by Elise Matthesen. Copyright © 1993 by Elise Matthesen. First appeared in *Xanadu*, selected and edited by Jane Yolen and Martin Greenberg (Tor Books, 1993). Reprinted by permission of the author.

"The Wife's Story" by Ursula K. Le Guin. Copyright © 1982 by Ursula K. Le Guin; first appeared in the author's collection *The Compass Rose*; reprinted by permission of the author and the author's agents, the Virginia Kidd Agency, Inc.

Every reasonable effort has been made to properly acknowledge ownership of all material used. Any omissions or mistakes are not intentional and, if brought to the publisher's attention, will be corrected in future editions.

Photo and Art Credits